"I knew exactly what I was doing."

He never let his mind get that clouded from anything. Remaining in control in every situation was how he'd gotten through some of the most difficult times in his life and how he had such a successful ranch.

"I wanted you. Plain and simple."

Her eyes widened, her mouth dropped to a perfect O. He couldn't tear his eyes away from that mouth... painted a pale pink today, but he'd kissed the hell out of it when it'd been siren red.

Just the thought of all the things they'd done had him wondering why they'd agreed it shouldn't happen again. The way she looked at him, the way she'd responded to his touch...

"I'm pregnant."

Ryan jerked at the bomb she'd set off right between them. Had he heard wrong? Was she serious?

One look at her face and he knew...this was no joke. He was going to be a father.

* * *

One Christmas Night
by Jules Bennett
is part of the
Texas Cattleman's Club:
Ranchers and Rivals series.

Dear Reader,

Are you ready for more scandal and secrets? I hope so, because Ryan and Morgan are here! Did you catch them at the masquerade ball? There were consequences to that night, and you're about to find out what they are.

I don't know about you, but I love a good holiday read. Throw in a few secrets and hot nights, and I'm hooked. And enemies to lovers is one of my favorite tropes of all time. There's a fine line between love and hate...or so the saying goes. I believe Ryan and Morgan are about to put that theory to the test.

I hope you're enjoying all of the amazing books in this installment of the Texas Cattleman's Club. I'm thrilled to be part of such a strong, dynamic series and cannot wait for you to see what happens next in Royal, Texas. So, grab your favorite cozy blanket, your drink of choice and settle in for *One Christmas Night*.

Happy reading!

Jules

JULES BENNETT

ONE CHRISTMAS NIGHT

Special thanks and acknowledgment are given to Jules Bennett for her contribution to the Texas Cattleman's Club: Ranchers and Rivals miniseries.

DESIRE

Recycling programs for this product may not exist in your area.

ISBN-13: 978-1-335-58150-1

One Christmas Night

Copyright © 2022 by Harlequin Enterprises ULC

For questions and comments about the quality of this book, please contact us at CustomerService@Harlequin.com.

Harlequin Enterprises ULC
22 Adelaide St. West, 41st Floor
Toronto, Ontario M5H 4E3, Canada
www.Harlequin.com

Printed in U.S.A.

USA TODAY bestselling author **Jules Bennett** has published over sixty books and never tires of writing happy endings. Writing strong heroines and alpha heroes is Jules's favorite way to spend her workdays. Jules hosts weekly contests on her Facebook fan page and loves chatting with readers on Twitter, Facebook and via email through her website. Stay up-to-date by signing up for her newsletter at julesbennett.com.

Visit her Author Profile page at Harlequin.com, or julesbennett.com, for more titles.

You can also find Jules Bennett on Facebook, along with other Harlequin Desire authors, at Facebook.com/harlequindesireauthors!

Michael,
I could dedicate all the books to you
and that would still not be enough
to express my love.
Yours Forever, Jules.

One

This could not be happening. Of all the slaps of reality, this one hit the hardest.

Morgan Grandin gripped the edge of her vanity top in the bathroom of her boutique, the Rancher's Daughter. Out of all the Grandin clan, she was the only one who never wanted to be part of that ranch life, so she'd paid homage by giving her boutique an appropriate name.

And if her family didn't like the fact she wasn't part of the family business, they certainly wouldn't like this next chapter of her life.

Morgan stared down at two blue lines. This was certainly not the way she'd planned on starting her Monday morning...or her own family. She'd always been the odd woman out as far as the Grandins went, but this would definitely make her even more of a standout.

From the moment she saw those two lines, she wanted this baby. But she had to look forward and formulate a plan that would suit her and her child's needs. What a mess she'd gotten herself into.

After washing her hands and drying them, Morgan glanced at herself in the gold-framed mirror. Well, she didn't look any different. Shouldn't she look…motherly?

She turned to the side, staring at her flat stomach. Both amazed and terrified, she imagined the little life growing inside of her.

How could she make this work being a business owner and a single mother? She wasn't married. She was also unlike her siblings, who had all found love and were living their own happily-ever-afters.

No, Morgan had opted for a drunken fling with the one man who drove her absolutely crazy—both in bed and out.

On a groan, she smoothed her red hair over her shoulder. All of this information couldn't be processed at once. She still had a store to maintain and customers to assist. This wasn't just some hobby she had, this store was her dream. She'd have to keep her little secret until she could get a grasp on her new reality.

For now, she couldn't even bring herself to tell her siblings…and she sure as hell couldn't tell Ryan

Carter until she gathered her composure and her thoughts.

One night. They had one night and now their entire lives were changed. The dynamics within her own family would change, too. Everything would be different from this moment forward.

While her siblings were falling in love, Morgan opted for a one-night stand with her enemy.

Before that night, she couldn't even stand Ryan— how in the world could she raise a child with him? They'd never agree on anything from choosing the name to choosing a school.

How could they be so completely different, yet be so perfectly in sync in the bedroom? That night had been nothing short of magical and memorable. Every touch, every kiss, was all she had thought of for the past month.

Oh, they'd both agreed that night would never happen again and they weren't to speak of it. She'd been on board with that because who would believe she hooked up with Ryan Carter? The entire town had seen them either bickering or snubbing each other.

And while part of her regretted that night, the other part ached for round two. Ryan had been the most attentive lover and the only man to ever make her want to sneak around for more.

At this point, though, she had to be smart about any decision she made. She wasn't just thinking for herself anymore.

Morgan pulled in a deep breath and stepped from

the bathroom of her boutique. She couldn't hide in here forever. Reality wouldn't change simply because she didn't want to face it. She took pride in her shop and that wouldn't stop or slow down now.

But who would run the place when she was off having a baby? Or if the baby got sick? She had a young college girl, Kylie, who worked here as she took online classes that one day would launch her career in fashion design. Morgan knew without a doubt that she could depend on her, but this store was everything to Morgan. While she could definitely afford to take time off, or even not work altogether, Morgan wanted to work. She loved being hands-on and socializing with the women of the town. She couldn't just unload this place onto someone else.

Morgan made her way to the front of her store and forced the worries to the back of her mind.

One day at a time. That was all she could do right now.

She flicked the lock on the double doors and propped them open, letting in much-needed sunshine. She inhaled the crisp winter air as she set her sidewalk sign out in front of her shop. The cool rush actually felt good on her heated skin. She hadn't realized just how worked up she'd gotten, but her nerves and emotions were all over the place.

Thankfully, though, she wasn't sick…yet. Good grief, when would that happen? So far, her cycle was off and she was emotional for no reason and she was only a month into this pregnancy.

Morgan turned and hit something hard. No, not something…someone.

Firm hands gripped her arms in an attempt to steady her and she reached out, encountering a very solid chest. She knew that chest. No amount of alcohol during their heated night could make her forget exploring such excellent muscle tone.

"You okay?"

Ryan's low voice caressed her, sending her nerve endings tingling. She could not, *would not*, be attracted to him. Their bickering had gone on for so long, that had to trump their one night of passion. The only time they seemed to get along was when their clothes came off and too much champagne was involved. Clearly neither of those things were happening again.

Vic always said how Ryan was a grumpy bastard who never said much, but he always had plenty to say when arguing with her.

"I'm fine. Just fine." Morgan stepped back and dropped her hands. "Everything's fine."

Shut up.

"Good to hear." Ryan smirked, his blue eyes shone bright with amusement. "You've been avoiding me."

"Have I?" she asked with a shrug. "Don't take it personal. I thought we agreed not to see each other again."

And if there was no pregnancy, she could hold tight to that promise. The sexual tension between them had bubbled for too long. What she'd always thought of as annoyance had clearly been attraction.

The night of the Halloween Masquerade Ball at the Texas Cattleman's Club and all the flowing champagne had been a powerful combination forcing them together—not to mention Morgan had overheard her brother discussing how Ryan was attracted to her.

The end result had been the most intense, memorable night of pleasure in her life.

But now she had to face the consequences. *They* would have to face the consequences. What label could they put on each other now? Enemies? That seemed a bit harsh, all things considering. As much as he deserved to know, now wasn't the time.

"Royal isn't that big of a town," Ryan told her, oblivious to her inner turmoil. "I always saw you around, but over the last month, you've been scarce."

She pointed toward the open doors of her shop. "I've been right here, so you weren't looking too hard."

Ryan's piercing stare sent a shiver through her. That stare had hit her so many times over the years. More often than not, she'd been irritated by those bright eyes beneath his Stetson, yet other instances she'd had a stirring of something she couldn't describe…or maybe she just didn't want to. She'd pushed aside any unwanted attraction because Ryan Carter could not be the man for her. The idea was simply absurd.

Yet she'd overheard her brother Vic and his best

friend, Jayden, discussing Ryan at the party. In fact, they'd specifically mentioned Ryan's attraction to her, which had taken her off guard. He'd never shown her that attraction, unless his grumblings counted as flirting.

Morgan certainly wouldn't deny Ryan's sex appeal, but he drove her crazy. All of that arrogance and how he was so damn opinionated really grated on her nerves. They argued about everything from how they ordered their coffee to life on the ranch. She could almost guarantee whatever her viewpoint was, his would be the opposite.

But the man knew when to shut up and exactly what to do in the bedroom…which nearly overrode his negative qualities.

She never would have made a move if her brother hadn't planted that proverbial bug in her ear. She should never listen to gossip or eavesdrop. Look where that got her.

Ryan tipped his black hat and looped his thumbs through his belt loops. That was another thing about him. The man was consistently boring with his wardrobe. Jeans, black T-shirt, cowboy boots, hat. Simple and plain. No suits for this cowboy and he made no apologies that he didn't do fussy. He might own a twelve-thousand-acre ranch, but you'd never know by looking at him that he had so much wealth and power.

The yawn of silence agitated her, as did those piercing blue eyes.

"Why are you staring at me?" she asked. "Don't you have somewhere to be?"

"What if I came here to see you?"

A knot formed in her belly. "Did you?"

He shook his head. "I was actually meeting someone at the coffee shop, but had to park down the street."

Royal did have a bustling downtown area and she was lucky enough to have the Rancher's Daughter boutique right in the heart of it all. Of course, that also meant running into everyone whether she wanted to see them or not. And right now, she wasn't ready to deal with Ryan or her hormones.

Aside from the fact she now carried his child, Morgan hadn't mentally recovered from their night together. Every delicious moment seemed to be on repeat in her mind. Even when Ryan hadn't been with her, he'd never been far.

And now, she would be bound to him forever.

Ryan couldn't figure out why Morgan seemed so standoffish. She'd jerked away from him immediately when she'd seen who had caught her before she fell.

And now she would not look him in the eye. Interesting.

Maybe that spark between them hadn't diminished, even though they'd agreed on only the one night.

Had she thought of him since the Masquerade Ball? He hadn't seen her at the Texas Cattleman's

Club since then and had started to wonder if he should text or call. He'd never been a clingy guy and never, ever begged for a woman's attention…but damn if he couldn't get that night out of his head.

Shouldn't he have gone back to being irritated at her by now? They were at odds every single day before their intimate encounter and he had no idea why he couldn't slide back into that mindset. He loved going toe-to-toe on any subject just to see how feisty her temper could get when he won the argument.

But he'd been exposed to a completely different side of Morgan and now he couldn't get that vulnerable, sexy woman out of his mind.

They'd not only agreed to the one night, afterward they'd both agreed it was a mistake. They weren't right for each other and neither of them was looking to get into a relationship. Life on his ranch was busy and that was where he devoted his time. It was the only commitment he wanted at this point in his life. Besides, one drunken night didn't lead to a permanent commitment.

Still, he wouldn't mind a little fling with the sexy shop owner, but she looked like she'd rather be anywhere else than chatting with him right now.

Was she having that much regret over what they did? Granted, the night hadn't been planned and a little too much champagne had been involved, but considering they'd been together a month ago and he still thought about it every single day…that was simply too much to ignore.

Yet, getting caught up in that short period of time would only prove to be a disaster. He had to get his head on straight and forget how perfectly they went together...because this was reality.

"I need to go back inside."

She pulled her green cardigan tighter around her body and scurried away, leaving Ryan more confused than ever. Morgan wasn't a shy or timid woman, she didn't play games, and she most certainly never ran away. What the hell was up? She hadn't argued with him or used that quick wit and sharp tongue like her typical go-to...which baffled the hell out of him. Who was this version of Morgan?

Ryan glanced inside the open doors and watched for a second as she took a few accessories from one display and put them on another. She seemed focused on work and going about her life, which is precisely what he should be doing instead of acting like great sex had changed his entire world.

Ryan checked his watch and pulled in a deep breath as he started on down the sidewalk toward the coffee shop. He didn't have the time to devote to something that happened weeks ago and he needed to clear his head space and concentrate on his ranch. With everything going on in this town from the weddings to the babies to the secrets, Ryan would do well to remember that he could get wrapped up in any of those disasters if he wasn't careful. That was why he avoided town as often as he could.

While he wanted to ultimately have a family of

his own to leave his legacy to, he certainly was in no hurry. When the right woman came along, he'd know.

So for now, he'd best keep his head down and his attention on the ranch. Nothing else mattered.

Two

Why were maternity clothes so insanely hideous? How could she incorporate a new line when she literally hated each article of clothing she'd been looking at? No woman gaining weight and losing her waistline wanted to wear the equivalent of a tent.

Morgan shut down her laptop, refusing to entertain anymore ugly clothes. She'd never carried maternity clothing in her store before, but with her wakeup call from earlier this morning, this should be an avenue to consider. Not to mention with half the town getting married and having children, branching out didn't seem like a bad idea.

Granted, she didn't need to take on more work to gain another demographic of customers. The Rancher's

Daughter had already well surpassed last year's profit and the year wasn't over yet.

It would take some time to figure out what to bring in, but perhaps she could launch her maternity section after the holidays. And, who knew, maybe later she could add an adorable baby line?

An image of little cowboy boots and gingham dresses popped into her head. Morgan glanced around the store and mentally reconfigured everything. Redecorating and looking forward to future sales and new customers was much easier than facing reality.

When she'd turned and plowed right into Ryan earlier, she'd panicked. She hadn't seen him since their night together and she'd had no idea what to say. Leading with "I'm pregnant" seemed harsh, though he would have to find out at some point.

What was the protocol for telling your one-night stand and sworn enemy that you were now bonded for life and he had eight months to get ready?

Morgan couldn't dodge him forever. Although Ryan likely assumed she was insane, the way she refused to look at him and practically ran back into the safety of her store. She'd just been caught off guard, that was all. She just needed a day or so to process everything, not to mention she should make a doctor's appointment to make sure that test wasn't a false positive. But she'd taken both in the box and had the same results.

And then there was that whole missed period thing.

Yeah. There was no denying what had happened

and the sooner she faced those facts, the better. She honestly didn't know who to tell first. Her family? Would they be disappointed or shocked or both? They already had so much going on with her sister's upcoming nuptials and the whole scandal with Heath Thurston wreaking havoc on the Grandins and the Lattimores. That man had caused an absolute nightmare requesting the largest estates in all of Royal to be dug up while he searched for his supposed inherited oil.

Morgan hated that her sister would be marrying Heath's twin brother, but there was no way to prevent love…or so Morgan assumed. She'd never been in love, and right now, finding love was the least of her worries.

She had to talk to Ryan privately, and out on the sidewalk in the middle of town hadn't been the place. Should she call or just go straight to see him? How would he respond to this life-altering news? Maybe he didn't want to be a father. What if he decided he wanted nothing to do with their child? How could she handle being a single mother?

All of these unknowns would surely drive her mad if she didn't get some control over her thoughts. She needed a plan. That was how she had such a successful business—she planned every last detail. Carrying that over into her now unsteady life would surely help matters…she hoped.

There were many people in her life she trusted and could confide in, but they were each so busy with their own lives, did they have the time to listen to her crisis? Her brother Vic would do anything for her, but she really would rather have a woman's perspective right now.

Of course Zanai would lend an ear and no doubt offer sound advice, but her best friend had just fallen in love, as well. Her world right now was perfect and Morgan didn't want to put a kink in that.

Morgan brought the new gold cocktail dresses from the back to put in the front window. Kylie had taken the day off, which was just as well. Morgan needed to stay busy and keep her mind on something else so she didn't have a total breakdown. Morgan planned on taking a couple days off this week, which would be perfect for her to mentally decompress and figure out her next steps.

She adjusted the shoulder on the mannequin just as the front door chimed. With a smile on her face, she turned to greet her customer, but spotted a welcome and familiar face.

"Hey, babe."

Her sister Chelsea came bouncing in with a wide grin. Of course the woman was overjoyed with life. She was marrying her true love, Nolan, in just a few weeks. A Christmas wedding was nothing short of fairy-tale material and Morgan couldn't be happier for her.

She really didn't want to ruin Chelsea's plans or their big day with a surprise pregnancy announcement. Maybe after Chelsea returned from her honey-moon would be better timing.

Morgan was just glad their family had come to-gether over the past month after Vic decided to share the ranch. Now the siblings were one unit again in-stead of divided.

"What's up?" Morgan asked, stepping down from the window display. "Are you visiting or shopping?"

Chelsea immediately pointed to the new dress in the window and gasped. "You didn't tell me this was coming in. Gold will be fantastic for my rehearsal dinner."

Morgan moved to the rack of new arrivals and lo-cated her sister's size.

"Go try it on." She held the garment out to Chel-sea. "I'll get your picture and put it up on my social media. You'll make the perfect model."

Chelsea rolled her eyes. "I don't know about that, and my hair is a mess."

"You're gorgeous all the time, now go." Morgan shooed her sister away. "I'll bring you this adorable strappy heel that also just arrived and you can com-plete the look."

Morgan went to the back and unboxed the new shoes, grabbing her sister's size. Just for fun, she also decided to get some accessories. If Morgan suggested anything to Chelsea, her sister would buy it. Might as well start padding that baby fund.

"I have everything ready for you," Morgan stated through the dressing room door.

"I actually stopped in to see if the things you ordered for my honeymoon had come in yet," her sister called back.

Oh, right. Morgan had every intention of looking that up…but her morning had taken a drastic turn.

"I'll get on that while you change."

Morgan maneuvered her way around the fat, circular ottoman and adjusted the folded plaid throws she had on display for the new home accent line she'd started carrying. Her cell vibrated in the pocket of her cardigan as she reached the counter. The moment she pulled out her phone, she recognized the number of a frequent customer and town busybody.

"Good afternoon, Sylvia."

"Oh, Morgan. Darling, I need to find the perfect dress for a Christmas party and I'm afraid I waited too long. Please tell me you have something in my size that will wow everyone and nobody else will be wearing."

Morgan tried to make every customer feel beautiful and special whether she was looking for a casual, stay-at-home outfit or a blingy, sparkly dress for a high-society event. She often ordered one dress so there were unique styles and no clones in this small town. If Morgan didn't have what a customer requested, she'd find a way to get it.

"I'm sure I can gather some things for you," Morgan promised. "Would you like to stop in and try on, or did you want an appointment after hours? Kylie will be taking appointments on Thursday for some one-on-one shopping."

In her midsixties, Sylvia Stewart always chose personal shopping, wanting to feel even more special, like she was the only customer. She also loved the chance to catch up on all the gossip she missed while traveling since retiring as Augustus Lattimore's secretary. Right now, Morgan really hoped Sylvia would choose her usual, because Kylie was an absolute pro at dealing with overdramatic shoppers.

"Why don't you pull them and send me some pictures," Sylvia suggested. "I'll let you know if I want to try one on or have you look for something to order."

Relieved, Morgan disconnected the call and immediately went to pull some dresses.

"What do you think?"

Morgan turned to see her sister standing at the opening of the dressing room. Chelsea stared down at the wrap style and adjusted her top.

"Do I look okay?" she asked. "I love it, but I always think things look better on other people than me."

Morgan rolled her eyes. "Oh, stop. You're stunning. I just need to know if you're thinking of getting it, because Sylvia called and needs me to put together some things for her."

Chelsea narrowed her eyes. "Don't you dare sell me the same dress you sell that woman."

"That's why I'm asking."

Morgan laughed as she took a few options behind

the counter and hung them in the closet area for her VIP customers.

"Did you get a chance to check on my order?" Chelsea asked as she put on the earrings Morgan had left for her to try.

"I'm doing that now." Morgan went to her laptop as Chelsea came up beside her. "I got a shipping confirmation for the clothes, but the shoes were on an entirely different order. Let's see where things are."

But the moment the screen came to life, Morgan's breath caught in her throat at the same time Chelsea gasped.

"Maternity clothes?" Chelsea asked. "You're going to carry maternity now? You've never mentioned that before. How exciting and great for the town with all the marriages and babies popping up!"

Morgan chewed the inside of her cheek, thinking of a proper way to respond. She couldn't to lie to her sister, but at the same time Morgan still had to process everything and she hadn't even talked to Ryan yet.

"Just thinking for now," Morgan replied honestly.

She quickly closed out of that tab, but the next one betrayed her.

"'What to expect in the first trimester'?" Chelsea read aloud.

Her attention immediately went from the screen to Morgan, and now Morgan had no way of hiding the truth.

"Are you pregnant?" her sister whispered.

"I just found out this morning," Morgan confessed. Some of that heavy weight instantly lifted from her shoulders. "Nobody knows, so please don't say anything."

Her sister's eyes widened. "Did you plan this?"

Morgan jerked back. "Planned? No, of course not! I'm just as shocked as you are. Well, probably more so."

Chelsea continued to stare for another moment and rubbed her forehead. "Can I ask who the father is? Do you know?"

Morgan sighed. "Of course I know, Chels. I don't just sleep around."

"I didn't mean that the way it sounded."

"How else could it sound?" Morgan fired back.

Chelsea reached for Morgan's hand and squeezed. "I'm sorry. I'm caught so off guard, I don't even know what to ask."

"I'm well aware of who the father is, considering I've had no social life for months and, bam, one time and here we are." Morgan pulled in a shaky breath and tried to not freak out, because speaking about all of this aloud made the entire situation sink in. "I haven't told him yet. You're the only person who knows."

Chelsea tipped her head. "It's Ryan, isn't it?"

"What makes you say that?"

"Are you kidding? The whole town saw the way you two were kissing at the masquerade party at the clubhouse before you snuck out. When two people are typically arguing and at odds, then they do a complete one-eighty, it draws attention." Chelsea shrugged and quirked a perfectly arched brow. "I'm just doing the math and coming up with the fact that was a month ago."

Wonderful. The moment people discovered she was pregnant, they'd immediately know also. That party had been amazing. Morgan had loved her mask she had special ordered with all the beading, feathers and bling. Every member of the TCC had been in attendance, but her friend Zanai really stole the show with her special makeover before the event. She'd always been a beautiful woman, but just needed a boost of confidence. The Masquerade Ball had been the perfect opportunity for Zanai to show her true self, which gave her the edge she needed to win the heart of Jayden Lattimore.

The night had been absolutely magical with the dancing and laughter...and Ryan.

She couldn't ignore the fact she still thought about him, about what they'd shared. But an intimate fling wasn't exactly the solid base needed for parenting skills...and that didn't even factor in all of the fiery arguments they'd had in the past.

"When are you going to tell him?" Chelsea went on, obviously drawing her own conclusion without Morgan confirming.

She shifted back to the laptop and closed out the telling tab. As she worked on finding the whereabouts of her sister's order, Morgan shook her head.

"I honestly don't know," she admitted. "We're not in a relationship, so I don't want him to think I'm ex-

pecting something from him. I mean, I can clearly
financially handle a child."

"I've no doubt, but Ryan is going to want to be in
the baby's life."

Morgan opened her mouth, but before she could
say anything else, the door on the shop chimed as
another customer came through.

"Not a word to anybody," Morgan murmured. "I'll
keep you posted, but for now it's just us. Not even
Layla. Got it?"

Morgan wanted to tell her other sister, Vic, her
parents and grandma in person. She just needed the
time to process everything herself before she took
it to the entire family.

Chelsea nodded. "I'll take this dress with the shoes
and accessories you picked out for me."

As she slipped back to the dressing room, Morgan
went to assist her customer and wondered just how
long this secret would remain so hush-hush.

Three

The sign in the window said Closed, but she was still in there. Ryan had seen her sporty little car parked in the usual spot.

Morgan's behavior this morning had plagued him the entire day. He'd been riding the fence lines and trying to focus on what his ranch foreman had been saying, but all Ryan could think about was how the Morgan from this morning was quite different from the Morgan he'd always known.

Sex wouldn't have made her so agitated and leery. The last time he'd seen her, they'd agreed they wouldn't mention having sex ever again, but did that mean they were never speaking at all? He'd almost rather go back to their verbal sparring matches than to have silence.

He wasn't a chatty guy unless he was arguing with Morgan. He realized now that every single time they'd quarreled, she'd been damn sexy.

Who knew anger could be so arousing? Maybe the line between irritation and passion was narrower than he'd ever thought.

Ryan never backed down from a challenge and he demanded honesty from those around him. He'd learned early on in life that people treated you the way you allowed them to.

He wouldn't let Morgan hide whatever it was that bothered her. If she just didn't want to talk, fine, but he had a sinking feeling there was something else going on.

Had he done something? He thought they'd both had a pleasurable night and were in agreement when they parted ways, but now…

Their one-night stand came on the coattails of years of frustrations and arguments. He had no clue what the next steps should be, but he needed to figure that out in the next few seconds.

Ryan spotted Morgan through the double glass doors and tapped his knuckles on the frame. When she spun around and caught his gaze, she simply stared for a moment. Time seemed to stop and he wondered if she was going to ignore him or let him in. He waited maybe only a few seconds, but it seemed much longer as those striking blue eyes stared back.

Damn. He could get lost in those baby blues, but

he'd vowed long ago to never lose himself in a woman again.

After being jilted and finding time to heal properly, he knew this version was stronger than ever before. No matter the relationship, whether friendship or intimacy, he demanded honesty and he had to remain in control. That was the only way he could keep his heart guarded.

Sure, Ryan could have texted Morgan, but he wanted her to look him in the eye because she'd refused earlier. He wanted to read her body language and if he had done something, then he would apologize in person to show respect.

And, fine. He wanted to see her. So what? Maybe he needed to see if they would revert back to arguing or if something else had sparked between them.

Morgan was a striking, intriguing woman he couldn't get out of his damn mind. For the past month he'd replayed that night over and over.

Vic and Jayden had put that stupid thought in his head about Morgan being attracted to him at the Masquerade Ball. Maybe she had been, but if she still was, she was clearly confused and reacting completely out of character. He had to see for himself now that no alcohol was involved and time had lapsed.

Finally, Morgan made her way toward him and flicked the lock. She eased the door open as she narrowed her eyes. Ah, yes. There she was. That spitfire he found way too damn appealing.

"We're closed."

"Clearly. We need to talk."

Her eyes widened a fraction. Was that fear? Hesitation?

Something was definitely up with her and he wasn't leaving until he figured out what happened to make such a bold, strong woman react so out of character.

"I was just getting ready to leave."

Again, she wouldn't meet his gaze up close. Ryan certainly didn't want to make her uncomfortable, but he did want to know if he'd offended her or hurt her in some way. Morgan never backed down from anything, especially an opportunity to tell him exactly what was on her mind.

Ryan slid his finger beneath her chin and tipped her head up so she had nowhere else to look. Her sharp intake of breath didn't stem from fear…no, that was desire looking back at him.

There was his answer. He didn't know why that revelation made him so happy.

"Are you letting me in or are we going to talk like this for the town to see?" he asked.

Her eyes darted over his shoulder, then back to him. She took a step back and eased the door wider, gesturing him inside.

Ryan glanced around at the stylish decor that combined modern metals with rustic Southern charm. There seemed to be so much inventory, yet everything had a neat, orderly vibe.

He turned to face her as she locked the door once again.

"I've never actually been in here," he admitted. "You've got an impressive place. No wonder it's so successful."

Morgan remained by the door and nodded. "Thank you. I never really wanted to be part of the ranch and this was always a dream of mine, much to my family's dismay."

"They have to be proud of your accomplishments."

"I suppose they are now that they see this isn't a hobby and I work as hard as they do. I just prefer people and fashion to cattle and spurs."

Ryan waited for her to move or speak or anything to break this tension that seemed to surround them. Being alone with her, having her so close physically but so far mentally, confused him. She was the sexiest woman he'd ever seen and there was no way to deny the pull that still tugged at him. Even after an entire month with no contact, he was just as mesmerized and turned on as ever.

"Do you want to tell me what has you so spooked?" he finally asked, breaking the ice.

"Spooked?"

Ryan shrugged and hooked his thumbs through his belt loops as he widened his stance. He figured he wasn't going anywhere for a while. They would either argue or tear each other's clothes off…he just had to wait and see which one.

"Something about me or what happened between us has you afraid," he clarified. "Did I do something or offend you in any way? Other than our usual bickering, that is."

"Offend me? No, of course not. You might annoy the hell out of me, but you'd never purposely hurt me."

Relief hit him and he realized he'd been holding his breath. He never wanted to hurt or disrespect any woman…despite what he'd been through in his past.

Morgan demanded respect and that was what she deserved.

"I know we said that night shouldn't have happened," he started. "But it did and ignoring it seems to be making things more awkward. I can't even get you to bicker with me anymore. I miss winning every argument."

Morgan didn't even crack a smile at his lame joke. Instead, she chewed on her bottom lip as her eyes darted down to her boots. He couldn't help but notice that instant difference between them. His well-worn boots likely had dirt on the bottoms from the ranch and were definitely not a fashion statement. Her boots looked like she'd just taken them off the display and paired them with her knee-length dress.

Everything about her screamed polish and poise. She lived her life making beautiful things happen while he…well, he kept the ranch running with worn jeans that were twenty years old. He really didn't care about buying new things when the old worked perfectly fine.

"We can't go back and erase what happened." She

shifted her attention from the floor to him as she took a step forward. "We just drank too much alcohol."

"I knew exactly what I was doing."

He never let his mind get that clouded from anything. He'd gotten through some of the most difficult times in his life by remaining in control. He wouldn't have such a successful ranch if he let his emotions get the best of him.

"Having a few drinks isn't what made me sleep with you," he added. "I wanted you. Plain and simple."

Her eyes widened, and her mouth dropped to a perfect O. He couldn't tear his eyes away from those lips, painted a pale pink today. He also liked when they were red and he'd kissed the hell out of them. Maybe smearing her lipstick should become a new hobby in lieu of fighting with her.

Just the thought of all the things they'd done had him wondering why they'd agreed it shouldn't happen again? The way she looked at him, the way she'd responded to his touch...

"I'm pregnant."

Ryan jerked at the bomb she'd set off right between them. He must have misunderstood or something, but there was no way...

One look at her face and he knew this was no joke. He was going to be a father.

Okay, so she hadn't meant to blurt that news out there like that, but she hated secrets and she couldn't keep the baby from him any longer. Now that her sister knew, Morgan only felt it right to tell Ryan. She had planned on calling him and setting up some time to meet tomorrow, but when he'd tapped on her door moments ago, she knew the time had come.

And he'd only stopped by to clear the air. He probably regretted that now.

"Pregnant?" he asked.

Morgan nodded. "I only found out this morning, so I'm still in shock myself."

"But we were careful."

"I thought we were, too. I wanted to tell you, but I didn't know how or when. I guess there's no perfect time or place to change someone's life, but you need to know that I don't expect you to provide for me or the baby. Of course that's your right, but I am successful with a family that will support me and—"

"We'll get married."

Morgan froze and stared at Ryan as he removed his black Stetson and raked his hand through his hair. He tapped the brim of the hat against his thigh as he held her gaze, clearly waiting for her reply.

"I'm sorry," she snorted. "Was that a proposal?"

"It was a statement."

Anger bubbled within her, and Morgan crossed her arms over her chest and attempted to remain calm.

"First of all, your delivery needs a ton of work. Second, there's no way in hell I'm marrying you just because I'm pregnant. That's the most ridiculous thing I've ever heard."

Ryan's lips thinned. "It's not ridiculous. I always planned on having a family with children I could pass the ranch to in the future. And despite what you might think, I won't be part of my child's life just whenever I feel like it. I will be hands-on and that includes being supportive of you, too."

"I can take care of myself," she insisted. Wasn't he listening?

"I'm aware that you can, but you don't have to and you *shouldn't* have to." He held up his hand just as she opened her mouth. "And I'm not only talking financial. This will be emotional, as well. We're going to have to work as a team from here on out despite what either of us wants."

He set his hat back on top his head and continued to stare at her as if waiting for her to say something about that preposterous proposal. Over her dead body would she marry a man simply because they slept together and she carried his baby. That was not only archaic, that was a recipe for disaster. Why would she settle for a loveless marriage that would likely end up in divorce?

"I will be perfectly fine," she reiterated. "I'm glad to hear you want to be part of our baby's life, but that doesn't mean you need to be a permanent fixture in mine."

Ryan took a step, then another, until he closed the distance between them. In an instant, his familiar, masculine scent enveloped her and those blue eyes captivated her. She couldn't move, couldn't think.

"Maybe I want you with me," he murmured. "Maybe I want to protect you. Maybe I want to make sure you're safe, that our baby is safe."

He reached out and trailed a fingertip along her jawline, causing a whole host of shivers to race through her. Damn her hormones for betraying her.

"Are you going to tell me that you'd rather ignore the chemistry between us and skip to coparenting and maybe friends?" His thumb grazed her bottom lip. "Can you be just my friend after what we shared?"

That heated night full of passion and fulfilled fantasies had been well beyond friendly. Was it any wonder she kept scrolling through those memories? She had to keep reliving it because it had seemed like a dream. No intimacy had ever been that intense, that…memorable.

And now he was tempting her with more nights.

But marriage? She wasn't about to fall into that trap. They'd barely gotten along in the past—why did he think living together and playing house would solve things?

Her sister Layla recently married Josh, and her other siblings would be heading down the aisle soon, Chelsea to marry Nolan and Vic to marry Aubrey.

Morgan was clearly the only one being logical. Love and happily-ever-after seemed fine in theory, but in reality, did that even exist anymore?

Just look at her uncle Daniel, who'd had a fling for a few months with a young woman named Cynthia. He never knew she had been pregnant with his daughter when he headed back to Paris. When baby Ashley was three, Cynthia married Ladd Thurston and later had twins Heath and Nolan. No one ever said a word about Cynthia and Ashley's past. The web of lies and deceit was woven so tightly in this town, Morgan had to watch every single step she made so she didn't get tangled up in it.

Yet here she stood, fighting every emotion she had against temptation with her own secret pregnancy.

"I'm sure there's a space between friends and lovers we can settle into," she explained, trying to ignore the tingling from his touch. "We'll be parenting together, that's all. I'm not wearing your ring or taking your name."

Ryan dropped his hand, but remained right in her personal space. Damn that man and his potency. Why did she have to be attracted to him physically? If she wasn't pregnant, maybe they could revisit that evening.

But she was pregnant, and the fun times and careless ways were over. Now they had to focus and do what was best for the child, and that sure as hell didn't include a wedding. Maybe they needed to get back to arguing. At least she could ensure her clothes would stay on.

"I don't have to buy you a ring, and feel free keep your name if you want."

He stared at her like he'd just come up with the most logical solution. Morgan took in a deep breath once again and attempted to make sense of how her day had been a total roller-coaster ride from the moment she awoke.

Morgan shook her head and moved toward her checkout counter. She needed a barrier between them to gather her thoughts and get a grasp on common sense.

"I'm not marrying you," she repeated as she shut down her laptop and tidied up her space. "And if you were not being so territorial, you'd see this is a bad idea."

She moved her favorite gold pen, lining it up with the computer. Then she shifted it to the top, then the other side. Finally, she plopped it into her glass holder with the others.

"Are you going to keep fidgeting with that pen instead of looking at me?" he asked.

Morgan sighed and glanced up. She hadn't heard him move, but once again he stood so close. Too close. Close enough to touch, to kiss.

She seriously needed to get ahold of her hormones because she couldn't be selfish and take what she wanted. Having a physical relationship with Ryan at this point would only be confusing and likely make him think she wanted that marriage.

"I don't need to look at you," she countered. "I've already given you my answer. I'm not getting married, now or ever."

Ryan's blond brows rose and his tanned forehead wrinkled as he had the audacity to smirk. "Is that right? You're the only one from your family not married or engaged."

"And? What's that supposed to mean? Just because that's what they want to do doesn't mean that's what I want to do." Morgan crossed her arms over her chest and tipped her chin up. "They also all want to live the farm life and that's also not for me, which is another reason we aren't getting married."

"I wouldn't ask you to run my ranch," he scoffed. "I'm asking you to move in, marry me, and build the next generation of Carters. I have no motives to steal you away from the life you've created for yourself here. I'm not asking you to grab your leather gloves and rope cattle. I'm asking you to join me in a legacy I've created and can pass to our child."

Good grief, this man was totally serious. The only thing that gave her pause was that he was hot, he rocked her world, and he was stable in his life. But that didn't mean she wanted to share that life with him. Ryan wasn't a bad catch…if she wanted to catch someone. He would make a great husband, just not her.

She had to get him to the point where he understood or at least thought she denied the request for his own good.

"Listen," she began again. "We're not getting married just because I'm pregnant. One day you might actually fall in love and want to spend forever with that person. I don't want to be the one to hold you back."

"When I have a family, we will all live on my ranch and be one unit."

Apparently they were at a stalemate because there was no way in hell she was budging. She refused to marry, but even worse, to settle for a marriage out of some archaic obligation. They would be surrounded by resentment, and that was no way to raise a child.

"You think about it," Ryan added. "I don't need the answer right now."

"Are you listening to me? I gave you my answer."

He leaned in. His chest bumped hers as his mouth hovered a breath away from her own.

"You heard me as well, so here we are," he murmured. "Two people who are stubborn."

Another reason they couldn't marry. They couldn't stop arguing.

"I always get what I want," she volleyed back, more than ready to stand her ground.

In an instant, Ryan's arm snaked around her waist and pulled her body flush with his. Before she could even gasp, his mouth covered hers and that fire he'd ignited a month ago fanned to life once again. Morgan gripped his shoulders and couldn't help the way her body responded. No matter what her head said about common sense, she couldn't help the physical pull that swept aside all rational thoughts.

With his lips on hers and that strong hold, not to mention the hard planes of his body, Morgan was having a difficult time remembering why she'd turned down that oh-so-romantic proposal.

Ryan shifted, easing back just enough to brush his lips along hers. His hand settled over her stomach as he murmured, "Think about that marriage for our baby."

His abrupt release had her grabbing for the counter to steady herself. She watched as he walked toward the door, flicked the lock, and stepped outside—leaving her confused and sexually frustrated.

If he thought one heated kiss would sway her, he would have to try harder than that. Morgan refused to let her emotions guide her choices…that was how she got into this mess to begin with.

Four

Maybe he'd been too harsh, too demanding.

Ryan gripped his steering wheel as he headed back toward Yellow Rose Ranch. His plans today had been coffee with a contractor to discuss some remodeling of his guest house, riding the fence lines to check for weak or worn areas, then talking with his ranch fore-man about moving a herd to another pasture. He got two of the three done.

Running into Morgan earlier had put a spin on the end of his day. Now he knew why she'd been so cryp-tic. While he did meet with the contractor and ride the fence line, he sure as hell didn't have the men-tal capacity or the energy to discuss moving cattle.

Tomorrow he'd have to go back to the contractor and discuss renovating some of his main house, as well. Adding in a nursery close to the main bedroom would have to take priority over renovating the guest cottage.

A baby. He was going to have a baby. Well, Morgan was having a baby. *Their* baby.

The idea that he had a chance now at the family he'd always wanted thrilled him. He was going to have a legacy, someone to pass all of his land and his estate down to, and a new generation of Carters.

He'd almost had that lifestyle once, but it had all been ripped from his hands. He'd thought himself in love, but he'd been young and naive with stars in his eyes. He was older now, wiser, and he sure as hell didn't believe in love. What did that have to do with marriage?

With Morgan so adamant against marriage, he had to think she didn't believe in love, either. Her mind worked similar to his in the manner of business. They were more alike in that way than he'd ever thought before, so now he had a leg up. He would have to use that angle to his advantage to get her to see his way.

Of course, using her attraction wouldn't hurt, either. She'd been damn near ready to climb up his body back at her boutique. Just thinking of how hot she made him had Ryan really wishing she'd just agreed to his proposal and come back to the ranch. What did she have to think about? She hadn't given his proposal any consideration before she threw out her automatic rejection.

Why wouldn't she want to marry him? He took offense to that, actually. Because she was Vic's sister, they'd known each other for several years. They were damn good together in bed and they were going to have a child together. Many marriages were built on much less.

Maybe she hadn't wanted a shotgun wedding and perhaps his delivery could have used a little finesse, but in his defense, he'd been caught off guard. A pregnancy was definitely not something he'd been expecting. Ryan merely thought she'd been acting cagey because she hadn't seen him since their night together. He thought she felt awkward, but apparently she'd known that morning and had been afraid to say anything.

He honestly had no idea how Morgan was handling the news. He hadn't asked and he also hadn't asked her how she was feeling. He'd gone straight into self-ish mode because he'd instantly panicked and flashed back to seven years ago when his fiancée left him standing like a fool.

He'd vowed then to put himself and his ranch above anything and anyone else.

But that time period didn't give him the excuse or green light to be an ass. Morgan deserved better and he'd never win her over by being a bully. He had to rethink and regroup.

He'd won arguments with her before and all he'd had to do was think like her. She wanted to have the control, so all he had to do was make her believe she held the reins and he'd win once again. Because this would be their most important argument to date.

Ryan's cell chimed just as he pulled into his drive. He paused in front of the automatic gate beneath the arch that had the ranch logo and name on display.

He saw Jayden's name and tapped his screen. Ryan put the call on the speaker as the gate slowly slid open to give him access.

"Hey."

"Bad time?"

"No," Ryan replied.

"I just called to vent. You sure you're not busy?"

"Let me guess. Heath Thurston?"

"Damn straight," Jayden confirmed.

Ryan's best friend had always been a go-with-the-flow type of guy and never let anything rattle him. But this nonsense about Heath's claim of oil beneath the Lattimore and Grandin ranches had turned the entire town of Royal upside down and had everyone questioning everything they'd known.

Was it any wonder Jayden Lattimore was so upset? The idea of someone digging beneath a ranch that had sat for decades untouched wouldn't sit well with anyone.

"I'm just damn thankful the surveyor didn't find any oil beneath the estates," Jayden stated. "But Heath is still a pain in my ass."

Ryan pulled up next to the stables instead of going on back to the barn. He needed to unwind and a nice, long ride might do the trick.

"Heath was looking for what he thought was a serious payout with oil," Jayden went on. "Who knows what he'll do now that he is losing ground with his claims."

"He really needs to end this," Ryan grunted.

"Agreed. Nolan says Heath's heart is in the right place, but I don't see how. I'll never understand how those two can be twins and be polar opposites."

According to Jayden and Vic, Cynthia, the mother of Nolan and Heath, had oil rights deeded to her by the Grandins and Lattimores. Supposedly the oil sat beneath the two largest ranches in Royal—owned by the wealthiest families. Upon her death, the deed would have gone to her daughter Ashley, if she'd lived. Now it was with the Thurston boys, and Heath had been hell-bent on staking his claim since he'd found the papers in his mother's effects.

All that did was cause an uproar for the past several months. Having the Lattimores and the Grandins as enemies wasn't the smartest move, but Heath didn't seem to mind. Clearly he had his eyes on the prize—the oil.

Ryan killed his engine and rested his arm on his console. "How are things going with Zanai?"

"She's the best thing that's ever happened to me."

A stirring of something akin to jealousy coursed through him. Where the hell had that come from? Jayden and Zanai were in love. That wasn't an area Ryan ever wanted to venture into again. To open up and be exposed to such vulnerability seemed like a nightmare. Ryan was happy for his friend, though, and wouldn't say anything to degrade what he'd found.

"So, how is *your* love life?" Jayden asked. "Anything to report?"

No way would he be getting into this, especially now that Morgan carried his child.

And that was just another area he and Morgan need to discuss. When and how would they tell people? Time was not on their side and a baby clearly couldn't be hidden away forever. They couldn't even hide their secret a few months.

"Nothing to share," Ryan told his friend.

"Is that right? Well, I guess you'll tell me when you're ready."

Ryan didn't want to say anything more and give Jayden clues to what happened immediately following the Masquerade Ball.

"I'll let you go," Jayden told him. "I assume I'll see you at the Christmas party, right?"

"I wouldn't miss it."

Ryan disconnected the call.

The Christmas party at the Cattleman's Club was always the biggest event of the season. Now Ryan had to decide if he wanted to show up alone or if Morgan would be on his arm. If she went with him, everyone would know the status of their relationship had changed.

Clearly everything hinged on what Morgan decided she'd do as far as they were concerned. And that was where he came in. He owed her an apology for not asking about her health, he owed her an apology for assuming she'd just drop everything and be thankful for his proposal, and he needed to figure out how the hell to get her to marry him.

Damn it. Apologizing wasn't something he'd ever had to do with her. They'd run into each other at various events or restaurants, get into a quarrel, and go on about their way. Odd, but that was just their thing.

Apologizing would be a big move in this new path with their relationship.

Ryan stepped from his truck and headed toward the stable. He hadn't ridden Midnight in some time and his oldest, dearest horse was just what he needed to get a clearer picture of his future…and his potential bride.

Morgan scooted the raw edge table from the front of her store toward the middle. She had piles of clothes stacked all around the perimeter of the showroom and had rearranged twice already. She was tired, irritable, and she had a mess on her hands that needed to be put back together before she opened in the morning.

Right now she either wanted to call in Kylie for emergency help or sit in the middle of this pile of accessories and shoes and cry. She didn't even know which thing she'd be crying about, so maybe just a good blanket cry to get everything out would be best. Then she could be done and move on stronger than ever.

She really should have waited on Kylie to help her, but Morgan had needed to get some of her frustrations out. Her business she could control, so she'd always used this passion as her outlet.

Morgan stared at the table placement and hated this spot, too. She should just burn the thing and start from scratch. Maybe she needed to hire a designer to come in and have a nice renovation. Hell, while she was at it, she should change the name of the store. The Rancher's Daughter seemed so…simple.

Morgan blew out a sigh and rubbed her hands over her face. She couldn't very well change everything all at once. She was just irritated and scared as hell that her life was out of control right now. She was grasping at anything that was within her power to maneuver or change.

She hated feeling like she had no say-so in the path her life was heading down. But she couldn't go all crazy with every other part of her life, either. Now that Ryan knew the truth, she really should confide in Zanai. Her best friend would be supportive and just the shoulder Morgan needed to lean on right now.

Aside from the pregnancy, there was still a heavy dose of confusion. She couldn't keep up with going from bickering to ripping clothes off to pregnancy. No wonder she felt on the verge of a meltdown.

When Ryan left earlier, Morgan thought of little else other than that kiss. He'd purposely put that sexual thought in her head and he knew what he was doing. She wasn't going to lose control again… not with him.

Morgan's cell chimed and she turned, trying to remember where she'd set it in this disaster. The sound echoed again and she found the device beneath a stack of boot socks on her checkout counter. She really might need to call in Zanai or Kylie for reinforcements.

She answered her cell without looking at the caller.

"Hello," she greeted as she walked back toward the empty table.

"Are you busy?"

Ryan's low, sexy drawl stopped her.

"I'm still at the shop."

"At this hour?"

Morgan walked to her large, round ottoman where she'd shoved it near the dressing rooms and took a seat. She toed off her boots and figured she might as well get comfortable.

"I have a lot to do," she explained. "I don't just open and close. I have to restock, reorganize, change displays. Kylie is a great employee, but there's only so much she can do and at the end of the day, this business is my life."

"You need to hire more help," he suggested.

She had every intention of doing just that so she could alleviate some of the pressure and stress during her pregnancy, but he didn't need to know her plans.

"I'm not telling you how to run your ranch, so don't tell me how to run my store."

She crossed her legs up onto the ottoman and wiggled her toes. She would sit just a moment and then get back to straightening up her disaster.

"Did you call to give me business advice or did you need something?" she asked.

"I called to see if you wanted to come by the ranch tomorrow for dinner when you were done working."

Morgan jerked back as his question caught her off guard. "I'm not dating you, Ryan. I'm having your child."

"So we're working backwards. It's just dinner, Morgan. You have to eat and my chef will prepare something amazing."

"Ryan. I'm not coming to your ranch for dinner or as your wife and right now, I'm too tired for another argument. I need to work."

She disconnected the call and wondered if she sounded ungrateful or rude. She didn't mean to be either, but she didn't want to give him false hope, either. Other than really great sex and a baby, they had no common ground. Couldn't he see that she only meant to save them both from heartache down the road?

Morgan shot off a quick text telling him she'd made a doctor's appointment if he'd like to join her next week. The baby was all they could have in common and she had no intention of shutting him out of that part of her life.

She set her phone on the ottoman and came to her

feet. Stretching her arms and back, she pulled in a deep breath and glanced around to decide where to start. Things might not be perfect, but she had to get this store back in some type of order.

Her stomach growled as she headed toward her stack of V-neck tees. Ryan had mentioned dinner and she realized she hadn't eaten anything since lunch. Maybe she had a granola bar in her purse. She seriously needed to stay on top of consistent meals for the baby. Everything about her life would be geared toward her child from here on out.

She decided to leave the table right there for now and started folding and displaying her variety of tees. She could add the boot socks in a nice wire basket in the middle and put up some signage about her Christmas sale starting tomorrow.

After nearly an hour, that part was done. Now for the rest of the store.

Morgan turned to grab another stack of tees and jumped at the man looking through her front windows. No, not any man. Ryan.

Of course he decided to show up after hours... again.

Morgan stepped over her various piles and signs and around racks to make her way to the front door. She flicked the lock and had a déjà vu moment from a few hours earlier.

"I do have open hours, you know."

"I never asked how you were feeling," he said.

"Earlier, I mean. I didn't check on you. I can admit when I was being a jerk."

Ryan smiled, and her heart skipped. Great. This was not what she needed right now. She barely had time for a bathroom break, let alone teen-level giddiness. Besides, she wasn't used to this unexpected wave of emotions. Before, Ryan only got her blood pressure up. Now he stirred her arousal.

He held up a bag and ushered his way inside. "I brought food."

The aroma wafting by as he moved inside had her stomach growling again and she totally forgave him for earlier. Morgan closed and locked the door then turned to face him. He'd stilled as he glanced around the chaotic area.

"You not only fight with me, you get into it with your clothes, too?"

"You're hilarious. I'm rearranging and it's gotten out of control." She crossed her arms over her chest and cocked her head. "How did you know I was hungry?"

Ryan shrugged. "I didn't know, but when you said you were still here, I assumed you hadn't gone out for food."

"You would assume right." She started to reach for the bag. "Thanks for bringing me something."

He handed over the food and propped his hands on his narrow hips. Nobody should look that good in a pair of jeans, worn boots and a plain black T-shirt, yet here he was conjuring up way too many unwelcome feelings. She shouldn't want him when she'd already had him, right?

Except that was the problem. She knew just how good they were together and her lips still tingled from their earlier encounter.

"Don't you have a worker who can help?" he asked.

Morgan nodded. "Kylie. She was off today and then texted about twenty minutes ago to say she has to take care of her grandmother for the next few days."

He glanced around once again as if trying to decide to run or stay. Honestly, she loved her job, loved being hands-on in the business she'd built from the ground up. Yes, there were times like this when exhaustion settled in, but that was just part of any job. Had she worked the ranch life like the rest of her family, that would be no different. At least she'd gone into her dream field, so most days didn't even seem like work.

"Where do you need me?" he asked.

Morgan blinked and clutched the paper bag at her side. "Excuse me?"

He glanced around again and laughed. "You obviously need help, so point me in the right direction. Be warned, though, I know nothing about fashion."

He knew enough to know not to mess with a good thing. Casual clothes were clearly his sexy staple and all she'd ever seen him in. Even at the masquerade party, he'd had on that same outfit, but he'd put a black blazer on to match his hat. No suit, no dress pants or dress shirt...just typical Ryan Carter attire. The man made no apologies for who or what he was—and maybe that was just another reason why he was so damn appealing.

Arguing and walking away was so much easier than trying to figure out this constant pull toward him.

"I don't need help," she told him.

Ryan slid his palm over his stubbled jawline and held her stare. "You're still going to try to be stubborn in the middle of this mess when it's nearly nine o'clock?"

Morgan didn't say anything. Instead, she took the sack to her counter and opened it to see what he'd brought her. A chicken sandwich and some fruit. Her stomach grumbled again.

"Thank you for this." She took a seat on her small stool and pulled out her meal. "Time got away from me and I didn't plan on being here this late."

"Did you plan on turning your store inside out?"

She shook her head as she grabbed a fresh strawberry. "I didn't plan on that, either."

Morgan attempted to eat without looking like something from *National Geographic*. She tore into that sandwich and had it gone in record time, though. She also tried not to keep staring at the man who was wandering around looking at clothes, hardware, tables and the rest of the disaster. It was the second time he'd been in her personal space like this and he just seemed so…imposing.

Having him here in her little world was much too intimate and she honestly didn't know if that excited or irritated her.

Those broad shoulders and rough boots were so out of place. Even in the haphazard area of her normally posh and polished boutique, Ryan Carter had a commanding presence.

"So, what are we moving around?" he asked, turning back to face her.

"We?"

He propped his hands on those narrow hips and she had to fight not to remember how easily she'd wrapped her legs around them.

Focus, Morgan.

"You can argue all you want about being independent, but I'm going to help you tonight. You might as well tell me where you want things or I'll do it myself." He picked up one of the mannequins from the floor and held it up. "What size is she? I'll find something for her to wear."

Morgan couldn't help but laugh. He looked so absurd, but he was dead serious. He wasn't going anywhere and she needed the reinforcements. Nothing wrong with admitting that on occasion.

"Fine. You can help, but you are not choosing outfits or everything would have on a plain T-shirt and jeans."

A corner of his mouth kicked up. "Nothing wrong with that, darlin'."

Ugh. Why did he have to be so Southern and sexy? And why did she have to be pregnant with his child? Of all the men in the area that she could have had a fling with, she'd opted for Ryan Carter.

Thanks, champagne.

Once she finished eating, she came around the counter and thought about how she really wanted things. Since she had an extra pair of hands, she might as well take advantage.

She just had to remember that was all she should be taking advantage of from this man.

Five

Ryan waited for Morgan to decide what she wanted done. He watched as she walked around muttering to herself. Something about Christmas dresses and a sale.

Just as she pivoted back toward him, Morgan's foot got tangled in a pile of denim and she fell forward. Ryan reached for her, just as she fell. She landed against his chest, her hands gripping onto his biceps as that mass of red hair curled all around them both.

He recalled another situation where all of that hair covered him, but this was not the time or the place to start replaying that moment. Unfortunately for him, he never could get control over when or where those delicious memories popped up.

"You okay?" he asked.

Ryan shifted so he could maneuver them both away from the piles on the floor. Morgan straightened herself. Shoving her hair from her face, she gave him a curt nod.

"Sorry about that."

Her eyes were everywhere but on him again. They'd created a child and she couldn't even look at him? She'd had no problem in the past going toe-to-toe with him, and this sudden change in Morgan confused the hell out of him.

"Morgan."

Her eyes darted up to his now and he closed that minuscule distance between them.

"We're not swiping at each other and we're not lovers. Let's find something in between. We can handle this situation together, but you've got to relax."

The noise she made could best be described as something between a snort and a laugh.

"Relaxing is what got me into this in the first place," she stated. "I just… I can't touch you. So, no more of those sneaky kisses. Got it?"

"Sneaky kisses?" Now he laughed. "Honey, you weren't complaining last month or earlier today. But if you want me to keep my lips to myself, I will. You'll have to tell me when you want that to happen again."

"I won't," she retorted.

He doubted she'd stick to that claim, but he'd let her have this small victory.

"Are you angry about our night together?" he

asked. "Or are you angry that you can't get it out of your mind?"

Morgan's lips thinned, and her eyes narrowed. "I'm angry that you want to talk about it when we should both be moving on. Clearly, the only time we get along is when we're not talking, so we're going to have to figure out a way to communicate with our clothes on."

"That doesn't sound fun."

Morgan rolled her eyes. "I'm serious."

Yeah, he had been, too.

"I know we agreed that sex was a mistake, but I can't ever think a child is a mistake." He had to be completely honest. "And the more I think about our time together, the more I can admit it wasn't a mistake, either."

Morgan gasped. "Don't say that."

"I'll never lie to you and you need to know where I stand."

Those bright eyes of hers had a healthy mix of desire and irritation. There was such a narrow space between the two and she had an amazing talent of riding that line to keep him guessing.

He wanted her. Maybe he always had and he'd never stopped.

Unable to resist temptation, Ryan reached out and trailed his fingertip up her arm, then back down. He took her hand and lifted. Flattening her palm against his chest, Ryan kept his eyes locked on hers. He waited for any sign that she didn't approve; she had nothing but desire in her eyes.

"Your words and that look you're giving me don't match," he murmured. "Makes me think you're just saying you're not attracted when we both know that's a lie."

"I don't want to be," she corrected him.

And that whispered statement was all he needed to bank in his pocket of ammunition. Morgan's admission couldn't be taken back now and at least she was honest. That was one area they had in common, but commonalities weren't a high priority for him right now.

First, he wanted Morgan. Second, he wanted her to agree to his proposal and move into his estate. They could work out the rest later.

"Who are you fighting now? Me or yourself?" he asked as he hovered his lips near hers. "You're a grown woman with needs. We both want the same thing."

"Physically, yes," she agreed. "But everything else—"

"Doesn't matter. Not in this moment."

He rested his hands on her hips and shifted her around so his back was to the windows in case any passersby happened to look inside. She couldn't argue with him about the proposal and moving in if he kept that sweet mouth occupied. Guess he was going to go back on that promise of no more kissing.

Ryan stepped into her, lining up their hips perfectly and eliciting a soft moan from Morgan. She closed her eyes and sighed as her hands came up to cup his elbows.

"This can't work," she insisted. "We bicker all the time and sex isn't the solution. We have a child coming that we need to think about."

Oh, he'd thought of little else since he discovered he was going to be a father. But that had nothing to do with this ache he had inside for Morgan. If anything, that attraction burned hotter than ever before. Something primal and territorial had settled deep within him since learning the news.

Ryan feathered his lips over her jawline and to that sensitive spot just beneath her ear. She shivered against him as her grip on him tightened.

He walked her backwards with no clue where to go, but he sure as hell wanted out of the line of sight of the street. Even at this late hour, Royal always had busy restaurants and the last thing he and Morgan needed was more fodder for the gossip mill.

"Wh-what are we doing?" she whispered.

"Going somewhere private."

He glanced over her shoulder to the closed door that led to the back. Ryan had no clue what was in there, but he didn't care. They would be alone and that was all that mattered right now.

"Is this a good idea?" she asked, her eyes searching his.

Ryan reached around her and opened the door as he stared down at her. "If you want to stop, say so."

"But we shouldn't."

"Who made that rule? Because last I checked, we were adults." He took a few more steps until they'd crossed into the storage room, and the door closed behind him. "If you say no, we'll go right back out there and finish picking up. Just say the word."

Morgan closed her eyes once again and sighed. "Let's forget about reality. Just for tonight."

Ryan didn't realize he'd been holding his breath, but relief spiraled through him. Then he remembered her demand.

"I'm not allowed to kiss you," he reminded her. "I need your permission."

Her eyes flew open, then darted down to his mouth. In a flash, Morgan grabbed his face and rose up on her toes. She captured his lips and arched into him. Permission granted.

Finally. After a month of wondering if their fiery passion was just a onetime thing or if his fantasies lived up to the reality… Ryan was about to find out. The way Morgan came to life in his arms was a hell of an indicator that alcohol had nothing to do with their first heated encounter.

Ryan didn't ask again if she was sure. He'd asked already and she never said no. She also aggressively kissed him since they'd gotten back here. She'd made her answer clear.

So Ryan decided to take control.

His hands moved to the hem of her shirt and he lifted it up over her torso. Morgan stepped back enough for him to pull the material over her head and fling it to the side.

Soft red curls fell over her shoulders as those bright eyes met his. That familiar desire stared back at him, just like at the masquerade party, where all he'd been able to see was her eyes until they'd gotten back to his place and he'd stripped her bare.

Now he couldn't wait to have an encore performance.

She'd sworn she wouldn't do this…not again.

But how could she deny her wants? Who said this was wrong? Maybe they didn't have everything figured out in this weird relationship, but that didn't mean they couldn't be intimate. Morgan didn't even have the excuse of alcohol this time.

And it hadn't just been the champagne from the party. She'd overheard Vic and Jayden talking about how it was obvious Ryan was into her, which had shocked her. Morgan had just assumed she and Ryan were totally opposite and irritated each other.

Clearly, conversing wasn't their thing and they communicated much better in other ways.

Morgan didn't want to wait, or chat, or even think about this moment. She just wanted to live in it.

With quick work, she stripped down to absolutely nothing while Ryan watched with those hungry eyes that made her feel sexy and beautiful.

His heavy-lidded gaze landed on her stomach and

before she realized what he was doing, Ryan reached out and placed both hands over her bare skin.

A tremble vibrated through her at his strength and warm touch. She couldn't get enough and could possibly start begging.

"You're the most beautiful woman," he told her. "You're even sexier now that I know you're carrying my child."

She reached for the button of his jeans and before she could finish, he took control. He unfastened everything and shoved them and his boxer briefs down to his knees, then maneuvered until he could kick them out of the way. He grabbed her once again, this time on her backside as he lifted her up.

Ryan spun them, pressing her back against the wall. The spiral rush of exhilaration aroused her even more.

She fit perfectly between the hard wall and Ryan's firm chest. He placed a hand by her head and kept the other on her hip as he joined their bodies. Morgan cried out as whole host of euphoric sensations overcame her. This fast, frantic passion was still so new to her and she wondered if that thrill would ever wear off…or if Ryan would always be so incredibly potent.

Morgan gripped his shoulders as his mouth covered hers. He seemed just as needy for all of the connections. Knowing she had this power over him, to make him lose control, turned her on even more.

His hips jerked faster against hers and Morgan couldn't take it anymore. She tore from the kiss and arched against him to pull even more pleasure from his body.

"That's it," he murmured, urging her on.

Just as her climax slammed into her, Ryan groaned and trembled. She clung to him with her eyes shut, wanting to hold on to this feeling of pure bliss.

But moments later, their bodies calmed and she still clung to him.

"Don't tell me you regret this," he muttered.

She shook her head. "No. I don't, but I'm not sure it's the smartest thing for us to be doing."

Ryan helped her stand on her own as he took a step back. He reached up to smooth her hair from her face, then grabbed his pants and pulled them on. He left them undone, as if he wasn't quite finished with her.

Once he gathered her clothes and handed them over, Morgan dressed. The silence became too much, but she really didn't know what to say.

"This might not be smart," Ryan finally stated after a moment. "But I can't get enough of you."

Yeah. That was where they seemed to fully agree. She couldn't get enough of him, either. But getting along intimately didn't exactly make for a solid foundation for anything at all and outside of sex, they bickered.

So now where did that leave them?

Six

Was there a protocol for doing the walk of shame into your own shop wearing the same clothes from the previous night?

Morgan had gotten home well after midnight, couldn't sleep, and had headed back to the store well before she was due to open. Even though Ryan had helped her get the showroom from war zone to presentable, there were still touches she wanted to do. Plus, she just wanted to look at it with fresh eyes.

As helpful as Ryan had been—in more ways than one—Morgan had been a bit distracted and her mind all muddled when they were working in here last night.

First things first, she wanted to change her clothes.

She wanted something fresh and more in the holiday spirit. She'd gotten some new sweaters in and even though this was Texas, the weather had mood swings, resulting in chilly nights.

Once Morgan grabbed a new outfit and did a quick change, she went into her office and pulled her hair into a neat low bun and applied some lip gloss. As she stared in the arched floor-length mirror in her office, Morgan couldn't help but turn to the side and smooth her hands over her still flat stomach.

Surprisingly, she didn't feel bad like she'd heard other women talk about. Morning sickness hadn't hit and she hoped it stayed away. Her appetite had grown…and apparently not just for food. Who knew pregnancy pulled out so many hormones and emotions?

Morgan lifted the white sweater and eased down the waist of her taupe wide-leg pants. She still couldn't believe there was a little life in there. She'd never thought about being a mother or having a family of her own. In this town, marriages and babies seemed to be contagious lately.

Morgan flattened her hand over her belly and vowed that no matter what, she would put the baby first. Above all else, she valued family and even though she was terrified of being completely out of control with the unknown here, she also couldn't deny the excitement at the idea of a baby. Her baby.

Well, hers and Ryan's.

Morgan readjusted her clothes and tried to push

Ryan to the back of her mind, but damn it, he just kept creeping right up to the front where he didn't belong. She had her life going just fine and all set the way she liked it. Then he had to come along with that sexy black masquerade mask where all that had been exposed was that kissable mouth and those bright eyes. The champagne fountain had flowed a little too freely and the next thing she knew, they were back at his ranch and in his bed. Maybe not her brightest moment, but she couldn't change the past.

And last night had been about taking what she wanted because she needed to be in control of something in her life right now when everything seemed to be chaos around her.

She should have regrets, but she didn't. Ryan was unlike any other lover she'd ever had. But great sex and a child on the way didn't make for a reason to marry. She didn't love him and he didn't love her.

Maybe she was the only one thinking clearly here because love didn't exist for everyone…and marriages didn't always last. She refused to put her child on a roller coaster of instability simply because Ryan wanted to build a family dynasty.

Thankfully, she had several months to lay groundwork and get a solid plan in place. She and Ryan would just have to sit down like the adults they were and come up with a course of action…one that didn't involve a loveless marriage.

Morgan busied herself accessorizing the mannequins in the window and adjusting the draped lights to give the party dresses the best glow. She loved this new line and knew the women in Royal would flock to grab them for the upcoming Christmas party at the TCC.

Just as she stepped away from the display, Sylvia Stewart stood waving on the other side of the window. Morgan smiled and waved back, though inwardly she cringed at starting her day with the town gossip. Morgan truly wished Kylie didn't have to care for her grandmother. She could really use her at the store right now.

Morgan went to the doors and flicked the lock and opened one side for Sylvia.

"I'm a little early," Sylvia stated as she stepped right on in.

"No problem at all. I was going to have these dresses sent to you this morning."

Sylvia waved a hand and shook her head. "I ran out to meet a friend for coffee and just thought I'd take a chance that you or Kylie was here."

"Come on in." Morgan gestured inside the store. "Would you like another cup of coffee or water?"

"Oh, no, dear." Sylvia did another glance around the newly decorated area. "I'm fine. I do love how you rearranged the place. You really maximized the space."

"Thank you."

Morgan loved the new floor plan, as well. Ryan had played a huge part in helping with the heavy lifting…but Morgan would leave out that nugget of information.

"I had to make room for more stock," she added. "I'm always busier at Christmas so I just wanted a fresher look."

Morgan went behind the counter and opened the double doors to the closet area. She pulled the items for Sylvia and hung them on the raised stand next to the desk.

"Would you like to try them on here or take them and let me know what works for you?" Morgan asked.

Sylvia started toward the desk, but stopped and glanced down.

"Oh, what was that?" she muttered as she bent down. She came up holding something. "I hope I didn't break this. It was just there and I stepped on it."

Morgan focused on the item in her hands…and realized that was Ryan's watch. Wonderful. Had he lost that in their haste to get to the back room for sex or had it slipped off when they'd been moving furniture and displays?

"Oh, that must have fallen off a customer's husband," Morgan stated. "I'll set it back here and try to find the owner."

Sylvia turned the watch over and smiled as her eyes darted to Morgan. "Looks like the owner is Ryan Carter, unless someone else has the Yellow Rose Ranch logo on their watch."

But of course he had his own damn logo on his

watch. A man with an ego that inflated would do something as trivial as that.

"He's not the husband of anyone," Sylvia added with a quirk of her silver brow. "Maybe he stopped by to see you? After the way the two of you were hanging all over each other at the Masquerade Ball, I would have assumed you'd be engaged by now with as fast as the couples in this town are moving."

Why get engaged when you could bypass that and go straight to family life?

Morgan certainly wasn't going to give Sylvia any more information or ammunition than necessary about Ryan.

"He actually did stop by yesterday," Morgan admitted. "I needed help moving some of these larger tables and that display stand with the boots. Ryan is good friends with my brother and Vic is always looking out for me. Ryan happened to be free to assist and his watch must have fallen off during the move."

Sylvia's knowing smile and quirked brows didn't budge as she handed over the watch. Morgan laid it on the desk and would text Ryan about it later. For now, she had to divert the nosiest woman in all of Royal.

"So, what did you decide about your dresses? Trying on here or taking them with you?"

"Oh, I think I'll just take them. What about accessories and shoes? It's Christmas and I do like to splurge on myself, especially for a party. Will you and Ryan be attending together?"

Morgan couldn't help but laugh. "Ryan and I are just friends, but I haven't even thought about a date yet."

"You two were pretty friendly about a month ago." Sylvia winked. "Don't worry. Some girls need their secrets and that cowboy would be a great secret to keep. I won't say a word."

Oh, maybe not *say* a word, but she sure as hell would send out texts.

Whatever. Morgan was well aware people had seen her and Ryan kissing at the ball and they'd seen them leave together, as well. So what?

As Morgan gathered up shoes, jewelry and a few clutch bags, Sylvia decided to keep chatting.

"Is Heath going to be at your sister's wedding?" she asked.

"I would assume so," Morgan replied, taking a delicate gold chain from a display. "He is the brother of Chelsea's fiancée."

"I would just think he wouldn't want to be at an event filled with Grandins and Lattimores."

Yeah, Heath Thurston probably wasn't thrilled, but Nolan was his twin and he wouldn't let him down.

Morgan was all for family ties. She just hoped no animosity spilled over into Chelsea's life once she and Nolan were married.

"I'm sure he'll be on his best behavior at the wedding," Morgan assured Sylvia.

She made a few trips to the desk with boxes of

shoes and any accessory she could think of that would go with the chosen dresses.

"Let me bag all of this up for you and then I'll help you to your car. I'll wrap the jewelry and place it inside the shoe box that I believe will be the best pairing."

Sylvia beamed. "You are so good to me. I'll be sure to let you know something by tomorrow. You still have my credit information?"

Morgan nodded. "I do."

"Wonderful. And, for what it's worth, Ryan is quite a catch. You two would be a lovely couple."

Great. Just what Morgan needed, the validation of Sylvia. Morgan wondered just how long it would take for word to get out that Ryan's watch was on the floor of her boutique.

Seven

Ryan stepped out of the shower and wrapped a towel around his waist. He'd worked damn hard today on the ranch, but no amount of manual labor could remove last night from his head.

Several times throughout the day he'd wanted to text Morgan, but he didn't want to appear clingy. The last thing he'd ever want anyone to believe was that he was desperate. He wasn't. But he did have every intention of getting what he wanted. There was no way he'd ever let a chance at having a family pass him by for a second time. He had a legacy to protect and an estate he wanted to leave to his namesake.

Maybe that made him sound old-fashioned like Morgan claimed, but he didn't care. He wanted his child close and Morgan with him. Love didn't have to enter the equation. Not all marriages were based on such fairy-tale ideals. He wasn't looking for love and he knew she wasn't, either, so why couldn't they make this work?

He'd gone to her shop with every intention of talking her into marrying him, and they'd ended up naked again. Clearly they needed a chaperone because they couldn't even have a conversation without getting intimate these days.

Ryan padded through to his adjoining walk-in closet. One side was completely bare and he had no idea why he even used this bedroom. The massive closet seemed a bit over-the-top when it only housed a few boots, hats, tees and jeans.

The doorbell echoed up to the second floor and he stilled. He wasn't expecting anybody and he'd sent his chef home. Maybe a stable hand needed something, but they usually called or texted.

He could look at his cameras, but he'd answer the door regardless. Ryan hurriedly pulled on a pair of jeans and fastened them as he headed out of his room and down the steps leading to the foyer. He crossed the cool tile floor and reached the double doors as the doorbell chimed once again.

Ryan opened one side and Morgan jolted back, her hand going to her chest.

"Sorry. I didn't know if you heard the first bell."

Ryan rested his forearm on the edge of the door and leaned in as he took in her pretty little polished outfit. She'd put her hair up on top of her head and had minimal makeup, yet she looked like the sexiest woman ever. Perhaps that was because he knew exactly how she looked beneath those wide-legged pants and fitted sweater.

"I just got out of the shower."

Her gaze traveled down his bare torso, then back up, and she attempted to square her shoulders and compose herself. Too late. That familiar hunger had already flashed in her eyes and revealed her true thoughts. Apparently they weren't done with that aspect of their relationship...good to know.

"Sorry about that." She cleared her throat and went on. "I thought I could swing by on my way home and drop off the watch."

"Watch?"

She pulled a watch with a leather band from her pocket and handed it over.

"You had it?" he asked, taking the piece. "I thought I lost it in the barn or out in the field."

Morgan pursed her lips. "I didn't exactly find it. Sylvia Stewart found it. On the floor of my shop. I'm sure the entire town now knows that you were in my boutique and since you're not married, everyone will think you were there to see me."

"I was there to see you," he defended himself, dropping his arm to his side. He took a step forward and pulled in a deep breath. "And I don't care what Sylvia or her gossip monger friends think. We're allowed to see each other or anything else we feel like doing."

Morgan offered a soft smile. "That may be, but I do have a reputation as a woman and as a small business owner."

"I understand that," he told her, taking another step forward. "Your reputation isn't tarnished simply because I lost my watch in your shop. What did you tell her?"

"A portion of the truth," she stated with a shrug. "That you stopped by to help me do the heavy lifting because she had noticed that I rearranged, so it was an easy way to skirt around the rest of the story."

The rest of the story. That made it sound like there was an ending to what they had going on, but Ryan knew they'd just gotten started. There wouldn't be an ending, not as long as they were parents together.

Which only reminded him of another thing.

"Why don't you come inside and we can talk."

Morgan stared for a minute, then let out a burst of sweet laughter. "You're kidding, right? You're half-dressed and if I come inside, we both know what will happen."

"You're damn good for my ego."

"Oh, please." She rolled her eyes and shook her head. "Your ego doesn't need inflating any more. I'm just stating a fact."

Yeah, he knew that, but he also knew they had to have some serious conversations.

"We need to talk," he informed her. "And it's dinnertime so stop stalling."

Her eyes darted away and he knew he had her.

"Come in, we'll eat in the kitchen, I'll even put a shirt on if the sight of my mere naked chest is too much for you."

"Wow. You really are full of yourself." She threw up her hands and motioned for him to go inside. "I'll come in, but we are just talking…and not about this marriage nonsense. We can discuss the baby."

Considering the baby went hand-in-hand with the "marriage nonsense," he would have to be careful how he wove those conversations together.

As much as he wanted her physically, that would have to wait. There had to be more to them than sex and he would have to prove to both of them that they could be more than just bedmates.

Morgan took a seat on the leather stool tucked beneath the large island in Ryan's kitchen. As promised, he'd put a shirt on and now stood at the stove preparing…she really didn't know what.

"I didn't know you could cook."

He flashed that sexy grin over his shoulder and she silently cursed the nerves that danced in her belly.

That was just hunger pains. Had to be. She wouldn't still get all giddy over a smile after all they'd done—would she?

"I can cook," he informed her. "You can't live on a ranch and not know how to prepare food. There are too many mouths to feed. But I do also have a chef that comes in four days a week. He is phenomenal and you'll weep when you try his homemade stew."

Her stomach growled at the thought of anything homemade. It wasn't often she had time to do much cooking or go out to a nice restaurant. Even though she'd grown up in a home with a chef, she was typically out late or working and never sat down with the rest of the family.

"Nelson also baked homemade rosemary bread this morning, so it's fresh," Ryan added. "Perfect timing."

"I didn't mean to actually come for dinner. I'm returning your watch."

"You could have called and I would have picked it up at the shop." He reached over and pulled out two large bowls. "But I assume you wanted to see the ranch again and I had invited you today anyway. Remember?"

Oh, she remembered.

Morgan rested her elbows on the granite and didn't reply. While the Yellow Rose Ranch was certainly impressive, she'd grown up on a ranch herself. With her siblings and their staff, there were definitely those mouths to feed like Ryan had mentioned. But she'd never learned to cook well or for a crowd. There were always people in and out of her home, but their live-in chef had taken care of all of those needs.

Morgan didn't hang too much with the ranch hands and once she was old enough to make her own decisions, she distanced herself from that lifestyle. Vic never understood. Neither did Chelsea, Layla, or the rest of the family. Morgan had always had a different vision than working on a ranch. She understood the legacy and the importance of it, but at the same time, that didn't mean she had to follow in the footsteps of her family simply because it was expected of her.

And she'd keep making her own decisions now, too.

Ryan's log-and-stone three-story house with porches all around was something to behold. It sat right in the center of Yellow Rose as if he wanted to see all of his land from anywhere inside. The man might be a working rancher, but he was still a billionaire and certainly lived like one.

She'd been around this lifestyle her entire life and wanted nothing to do with living on a ranch. But now her world would be tied to his forever.

Perhaps she could have just called and he would have come by her store to pick up his watch. Ryan had been right in saying they needed to talk, but she honestly had no clue where to start.

"Can I do something to help?"

"Just relax." He busied himself getting drinks and setting everything on the island. "Were you busy at the store today?"

Morgan reached for her tea and stared across the counter. Ryan stared back, legit waiting on her reply and she couldn't help but snort.

"Is that what we're doing now?" she asked. "Pretending this is a relationship?"

Ryan took a seat across from her and reached for

his fork. "I'm not pretending anything. Just asking a question. I was busy riding more fence lines today and we have one mare that's about to deliver any day so we've been keeping an eye on her. One ranch hand didn't show up for work and decided halfway through the day to text that he wasn't coming back."

Morgan listened to him discuss his day and knew he worked hard. Her entire family were ranchers and the amount of work that went into running a successful operation could be exhausting.

There was something to be said about a hardworking man. They were loyal and very likely trustworthy. But she didn't know him well enough to fully trust. How could she? Before they'd fallen into bed together, all they managed to do was snipe at each other. How could she even consider a marriage of any kind if they didn't have a foundation of trust?

Ryan had always been Vic's friend, never hers. Until now. But were they friends? She had no idea what label to put on this unusual relationship.

Morgan pushed away the worry as she took her first bite of stew. The groan escaped her before she even realized. Then she took another and came to the conclusion Ryan's chef was a gift from heaven.

"Good, right?" he asked with a smile.

"I don't have the right adjective. I haven't even tried the bread yet."

"Nelson can turn a pile of ingredients into something magical and make it look so easy."

"He should open a restaurant if he can cook everything this good," she told him.

"He's not going anywhere," Ryan replied. "I overpay him for just that reason. I never want him to leave."

Morgan tore off a piece of the rosemary bread and dipped it into the stew. Oh my word, how could anyone be this masterful in the kitchen?

"Is Nelson's cooking reason enough for you to move in here and marry me?"

Morgan nearly choked on her bread. She reached for her tea and took a long drink, mostly to gather her thoughts.

"Well, you went a whole twenty minutes without bringing up your favorite topic." She took another drink, then set her glass back down. "I can visit, but I'm not living here or marrying you."

"I see no reason not to." He kept his head down and focused on his dinner like this was a done deal. "A child needs both parents and as I told you yesterday, I want to not only help the baby, I want to be there for you."

Morgan set her fork down and opened her mouth, but Ryan held his hand up.

"We've been through this, I know. Just hear me out."

Nothing would change her mind, but she would let him speak before she shot down his proposal once again. She'd been raised to be respectful, so she'd let

Ryan say anything he wanted while she enjoyed the most delicious meal she'd had in a long time.

"I spent the entire day thinking of a solution," he started. "Being selfish or controlling is not my main goal here. My goal is to have my family all together and be one unit. I want my child to grow up on the ranch and learn what real work is."

"On that we can agree," she replied. "I don't want my child believing he or she would always get money simply because we have it. I want them to work for it."

"So marry me and we can build this life with the same vision."

Morgan sighed and sat back in her leather bar stool. "A life? What kind of life is being trapped in a love-less marriage? You think you'd never want to date again or maybe find a woman you actually want to spend your life with?"

Ryan pushed away from his side of the island and came around to stand next to her. He placed a hand on the back of her stool and turned her to face him fully. Morgan swallowed at the intensity of his gaze. Ryan was completely serious about this situation and her words were not cutting through his hard head.

"I tried love once," he explained through gritted teeth. "I still have the internal scars to prove it. I'm here for the family and the legacy, that's it. You and I have chemistry, so why shouldn't we try? Live here for one month. That's all I'm asking. I know you want to challenge me at every point, but just give this idea a try and then decide."

There was no desperation in his voice, but an underlying command. He wanted this to happen. He wanted her in his home and very likely in his bed.

"You think I'll change my mind after a month?" she finally asked. "My stance will be the same. Neither of us deserves to be trapped in a marriage."

"I'm not trying to trap you. I'm telling you this is for the best and once you stay here and see that, you'll agree."

Ryan rested his big, strong hands on her upper thighs. The man was wearing her down with his home and hearth vision and that sexy bedroom stare. She could do much worse than having Ryan Carter demand she move in and marry him. The attraction alone tempted her. The idea of spending all of her nights with Ryan heated her body and stirred her desires. Maybe she should consider being with the father of her child. They could learn to make a unit, a family.

Morgan chewed the inside of her cheek as she thought of how to answer. He didn't lay out a bad option for the both of them to try this arrangement for a month. Perhaps if she stayed, he'd see that playing house wasn't all that fun. If she left a towel on the floor or snored too loudly or cluttered his bathroom vanity with her beauty bottles, maybe then he'd be ready to coparent while living apart.

"One month," she agreed. "At the end of that

month, you'll have to respect my decision to remain single and we can go back to our bickering like we're used to."

A corner of Ryan's mouth kicked up. "That won't happen, but challenge accepted."

He covered her lips with his and Morgan's belly quivered at the prospect of living with this potent, captivating man.

Without a doubt, the next month would prove to be memorable.

Eight

"You're doing what?"

Vic's voice boomed through the cell speaker and echoed in the boutique as Morgan continued to scroll through the new maternity line she'd been considering. She knew her older brother would be shocked at this news, but she couldn't exactly keep it from him.

"You heard me," she told him. "I'm moving in with Ryan."

"I get that, but what the hell for?"

Yeah, that was part of the story she really didn't want to share, but yet another aspect of her life she couldn't exactly hide for much longer.

"Well, that's something I'd like to discuss in person. Do you have time to run by the store? I don't open for another thirty minutes."

"Why do I have a feeling I'm not going to like this?" Vic asked.

Morgan clicked on an adorable A-line dress with pockets. "I don't know if you'll like it or not, but I'd rather not get into my personal affairs over the phone."

"I'm on my way."

He disconnected the call and Morgan went to unlock the front door. Vic was just down the street getting some supplies for the Grandin ranch when he called and Morgan had dropped the bomb. She didn't want him to hear about her living situation or pregnancy from anyone else and this would be news that would blast through town faster than a wildfire.

And as far as the baby news, she had to tell him. Out of all of her siblings, she had always been closest to Vic and she knew he would support her and be there for her no matter what. Besides, Chelsea already knew so this would only be fair.

Moments later, the chime on her door echoed and she glanced up to see her brother striding in. He adjusted his Stetson and made his way toward her desk.

"Spill it," he demanded. "What's going on with you and Ryan?"

"Well, good to see you, too." Morgan came to her feet and crossed to give him a kiss on the cheek. "Would you like to get some Christmas shopping done for your fiancée? I know exactly what Aubrey would love."

Vic propped his hands on his hips and glared at her. "Stop stalling and tell me what's going on."

She was stalling and he was about one more breath away from steam shooting out of his ears. Morgan clasped her hands in front of her and pulled in a deep breath.

"I'm pregnant."

Vic continued to stare and silence enveloped them. She waited for him to say something, anything, but he seriously just stared.

"You're joking," he finally stated.

Morgan snorted. "Is that really something I'd joke about?"

Vic shook his head and muttered something beneath his breath.

"What?" she asked. "Just say it."

"I can't believe you and Ryan are having a baby," Vic exclaimed. "When I... I never expected... I mean, you two were pretty into each other at the Masquerade Ball, but this is..." Vic seemed completely flustered.

"Yeah, that's pretty much how I felt, too. He wants me to marry him, but that's taking things a bit far. So we're trying to live together, basically to prove each other wrong."

Vic reached out and took her hands in his. "This is moving rather fast, don't you think?"

Morgan nodded. "Extremely, and that's why I'm not marrying him. We need to figure out the best course of action for the baby. But Vic, please don't say a word. We're not ready to tell people yet."

Her brother gave her hands a reassuring squeeze. "I won't say a word."

Morgan let out a sigh of relief and closed her eyes. "Thank you."

Vic pulled her into a tight embrace and she realized that was all she needed. Some comfort from her big brother. Just that simple gesture eased some of her worries. No matter what her future held, she knew Vic would always be there for her.

When she eased back, she couldn't help but laugh. "You know, this is partly your fault."

Vic cocked his head and adjusted his hat. "And how do you figure that?"

"Oh, I overheard you and Jayden talking about Ryan. I believe your exact words were, 'It's obvious he's into her.'"

Vic's smile reminded her of when they were younger and he'd get into mischief and then try to lie his way out of it.

"Well, maybe we embellished just a bit," Vic defended himself. "And none of this is on me. If you were eavesdropping, then that's totally on you."

"So you're saying you tricked me?" she scolded. "Are you serious right now?"

"What? We knew you were listening." He shrugged as if that conversation didn't change her life. "Everything will work out. You'll see."

Morgan tucked her hair behind her ears and moved behind her desk to take a seat. She couldn't go back in time and change anything, and being angry or irritated with Vic wouldn't get her anywhere, either. She had bigger issues and worries than her meddling brother.

"I know you share everything with Aubrey," she began. "But I'd appreciate it if you didn't say anything about the baby. We'll tell everyone, we just need some time. We're still processing and trying to figure out what we're doing."

Vic nodded. "Understandable, but when she finds out that I knew and didn't share, she'll be upset."

Morgan offered a smile. "Well, I'm sure she'll get over it and you deserve nothing less for planting that idea in my head. Besides, she'll forgive you and slide into the role of auntie very well."

Vic groaned. "Damn it, I didn't even think of the hit my credit card will take."

"Your credit card can handle it." Morgan crossed her legs and rested her arm on the desk. "I really appreciate you stopping in. I wanted to tell you, but I didn't know how or when. Then you called and the opportunity presented itself."

"I'm glad you told me. Just make sure you're doing what is best for you and the next little Grandin. No matter what Ryan wants, you have to look out for you first."

Morgan nodded in agreement. She knew at the end of the day, she would have to do what was best for her and her baby.

"I need to get going," he told her. "You promise you'll let me know if you need anything at all? No matter the time or anything. I'm here for you. Got it?"

Tears pricked her eyes as Morgan came to her feet and hugged him once again.

"Well, don't cry." He chuckled as he wrapped his arms around her once again.

"Damn pregnancy hormones," she muttered as she eased back. "Thanks for keeping my secret."

He tipped his hat and turned on his booted heel and left her boutique. Morgan patted her damp cheeks and went to the closest mirror to see if she looked a mess. She was a hideous crier. Red nose, red-rimmed eyes, splotchy skin. Must be her pale complexion that betrayed her when she showed emotion.

Morgan figured she was okay as she adjusted her long red hair over one shoulder. She did feel better now that Chelsea and Vic knew the truth. Next up was Layla, then Mom, Dad and Grandma. Luckily, Layla was busy with her new husband, and her parents and grandmother were visiting friends for the weekend. She wouldn't have to tell them for several more days.

First things first. She planned on taking a few of her things to Ryan's house later. He was meeting her at her family ranch after she closed so he could help her gather whatever she wanted to bring.

For the next month, she was going to play house with Ryan Carter and she only assumed they'd be sharing a bed. His bed.

* * *

"Looks like you're staying longer than a month."

Ryan stared at the suitcases and totes they had hauled over from her parents' house where she still lived. He would have offered for a few of his employees go gather her things and move her in, but he wanted to be discreet for Morgan's sake. He hadn't told a soul about their situation and until they discussed things further, he wanted to respect her privacy.

"No, this is it for a month," she informed him. "I have a lot of clothes, shoes and accessories. Plus there's the party at the TCC for Christmas and Chelsea's wedding. It looks like I packed my entire closet, but I swear I only brought necessities."

Five suitcases and four totes were necessary?

"Don't you own a store you could grab clothes from whenever you want?" he asked, turning to focus on her.

Morgan rolled her eyes. "I sell what I have to my loyal customers, that's the whole point. Of course I keep pieces, but I can't exactly go in every day and grab something new. That's not how a successful business is run. I would think you'd understand profit margin."

She glanced toward the wide staircase leading to the second floor and then glanced down to all of her belongings.

"Which room is yours?" she asked. "I assume upstairs."

"My room is upstairs," he confirmed as he took a step toward her. He lifted her chin and turned her to face him. "But you'll be in the room across the hall from me."

Morgan jerked back, her brows drew in, and she blinked. "Excuse me? We're not sharing a room? I thought that was the whole point of me moving in here."

Ryan framed her face with his hands and held her in place. He wanted to be very clear and didn't want there to be any confusion.

"You're here because I want you to see how we could be as a family. But we shouldn't sleep together, Morgan. We've done everything backwards, and for the sake of our child, we need to see if we can live together."

Morgan continued to stare at him and he knew his statement had taken her by surprise. Honestly, his stance shocked him, too, but this would be best in the long run.

Damn if it wouldn't be difficult being so close to her and not being intimate.

"You're serious."

Ryan nodded. "The room is all ready for you and you have your own bath with a large soaker tub. I figured that room would be best so you can relax after working all day on your feet."

Morgan stared another minute before she took a step back. She didn't say another word as she went to one of her suitcases and extended the handle.

"I'll get these," he told her. "You shouldn't be lift-ing anything."

She completely ignored him and started for the steps. "I'm more than capable of taking the lighter ones."

"Then you can wheel them to the elevator." He gestured toward the hallway. "But I really can get ev-erything if you want to go on up and check out your room."

"First thing you need to learn about me is that I don't sit by and watch other people do the work."

She wheeled the suitcase down the hall, then glanced around, and back to him.

"I have no clue where I'm going," she admitted.

"That would have been a more dramatic exit if you had." Ryan lifted two of the totes. "Follow me."

Making his way down the hall, he led Morgan to the elevator. Once they were upstairs, he started showing her around her room, hoping she'd get dis-tracted enough that he could go back and get the rest of the load.

"This bathroom is even bigger than mine and I didn't think that was possible." She trailed her fin-gertips along the edge of the marble counters. "Oh, my. Now, this vanity really makes me have some envy."

She pulled the faux fur stool out and took a seat. She stared at her reflection in the mirror and then noticed the bouquet of fresh cyclamens.

"Did you have these brought in for me?" she

asked, catching his reflection in the mirror as he stood behind her.

"I wanted you to feel like this room was for you," he admitted.

He wasn't about to tell her he'd had the stool delivered and the bedding completely changed out, and added a new white chaise so she could relax at the end of the day.

"The cabinet is stocked with towels and bubble bath. There's a variety because I didn't know what scent you'd like or if you were allergic to anything."

Morgan came to her feet and turned, but rested against the vanity. With her hands by her hips, fingertips curled around the edge of the counter, she tipped her head and looked both adorable and sexy. He had to take a mental step back and focus.

Yes, they were alone, but they also had to take charge of this situation and not allow their hormones to control them.

"You're seriously going to tell me that this big tub is all for me?" she asked, a corner of her mouth tipping up in a naughty grin. "That this big bed will only be for me and you'll stay across the hall in your bed? Am I understanding this correctly?"

Ryan nodded. "For this month that you agreed to, yes. If you want to stay after that and marry me, I'll have your stuff moved to my room so fast."

"You won't last a month with me under your roof with nobody and nothing around to stop us."

Why did that sound like a challenge?

And why did she sound like she was going to seduce him?

Damn. Maybe he underestimated his willpower
around this sexy vixen. That look in her eye said she
was hell-bent on proving him wrong.

Game on.

Nine

"What the hell is all of that?"

Morgan glanced up from her position on the steps and smiled at Ryan's scowl as he stood in the foyer looking up.

"It's decoration." She fluffed more of the fresh garland around the banister. "This place really needed to be more festive."

"I have a tree up in the living room. That's festive enough."

Aw, poor baby didn't like her putting her feminine touches in his domain. Too bad. She didn't like sleeping alone when the best lover she'd ever had slept mere steps away.

They'd rolled into day three of living together, and

she really didn't know how much longer she could go without his touch.

"Yeah, I fixed your tree, too," she informed him. "Those ornaments were pretty sparse. I added a few of my personal touches."

Ryan closed the door and continued to stare. Morgan came down another step and went about her decorating.

"Bad day on the ranch?" she asked. "You seem… cranky. Or perhaps it's sexual frustration."

"I'm fine."

Considering his declaration came through gritted teeth, she had to assume he was anything but.

"Nelson made meat loaf and mashed potatoes with fresh asparagus for dinner. If he keeps making such delicious things, I'm going to have to buy bigger clothes." Morgan stilled and then groaned. "I guess that's irrelevant at this point. I'm going to blow up like a whale anyway."

"You look fine now and you'll look fine no matter what size you are later."

An unexpected flutter filled her and she didn't want his compliments. She wanted in his bed for the duration of her stay and she wanted to figure out a solid plan for parenting. That was it. None of these extras that delved too far down into the barrel of emotions.

"Do you want to help with my idea for the exterior or should I ask TJ?"

Ryan sighed. "Leave my ranch foreman alone and

the outside is just fine. I'll throw a wreath on the front door if that makes you feel any better."

Morgan finished adjusting the gold ribbon wrapped around the garland, then came down off the steps. She made her way to Ryan, got within inches, and crossed her arms over her chest.

"Have you always hated Christmas or are you trying to be difficult?"

"Neither." He took off his hat and hung it on the metal hook near the front door. After raking his hand over his mussed hair, he propped his hands on his hips. "I just never understand why so much energy is spent on something that will be taken down in a short time. I celebrate the holiday and buy appropriate gifts, but I don't have the time to take for anything else."

Something was off with him and she couldn't put her finger on it. Even through all of their quarrels, he'd been a fairly easygoing guy. Ryan had always been cocky, a little arrogant and totally in control of his emotions. He made jokes at her expense and could seduce her with just one look.

This was a whole other side of Ryan and something in her wanted to figure out every aspect of him. When he had days like this, who did he typically talk to? His ranch foreman, his ranch hands, and his chef were all centered around business. Did he open up to Vic or Jayden?

"What happened?" she asked.

Ryan blinked and stared. "When?"

"Today. Something happened and you're upset."

Silence settled between them and she waited for him to say something. That intense stare he had gave no indication of what he was thinking or even feeling. Up until now, she'd been able to read him pretty well. But they'd also only had very intense relationships on each side of the spectrum. They were either arguing or passionate. They'd yet to find middle ground and that was precisely where they needed to land.

"It's nothing."

He started to turn and head toward the steps, but she grabbed his arm. Clearly caught off guard, Ryan glanced from her hand curled around his biceps to her face.

"Don't lie to me," she demanded. "If you don't want to talk about it, say that, but don't say it's nothing when obviously you're upset."

"Fine. I don't want to talk about it."

He pulled from her grasp and continued up the steps, muttering about the garland the entire way. Morgan watched until he disappeared and even then she continued to stare at the top of the landing.

Whatever he was dealing with likely had to do with the ranch. She shouldn't be annoyed that he wouldn't talk to her. She'd been adamant from the start that she didn't want more with him than coparenting and intimacy. She couldn't ask him to be all in if she had no intention herself.

Still, she couldn't explain why, but she wanted to be that person he talked to. She didn't want him to just keep feelings bottled up. How would that help anything?

He needed space and she needed dinner. Once he cooled off, maybe he'd want to talk. She just wished she didn't care so much. This was only day three and she couldn't even imagine how she'd feel come day thirty.

Ryan stepped from his bathroom to the adjoining bedroom and stilled. There on his king-size, four-poster bed sat a tray with dinner, tea and a note written on the napkin.

I'm turning in early. Hope tomorrow is better.
M

He stared at the note and her delicate handwriting. He was having a baby with the woman and had never seen her writing until now. There were so many little things he just didn't know and he had no idea what all he was missing, but he did know he owed her an apology.

The day at the stables had been depressing and infuriating. Most days he loved his job. He loved the manual labor of running a ranch. But then there were days like today when losing an animal made him realize the fragility of everything around him.

And instead of being thankful that Morgan was comfortable enough here to make the place her home, he'd shut down and lashed out.

Why was he always apologizing to her?

Oh yeah. Because lately he'd been a jerk. He never intended for her to be the target of his frustrations, but she was there and he seriously needed to get a grasp on his control.

He hadn't been in the shower too long, so perhaps she hadn't gotten in bed yet. He would just tap on her door, apologize and thank her for dinner.

Guilt niggled at him because he'd invited her here so he could take care of her. Even though she claimed she didn't need his help, he'd wanted to prove to her that they would be a great team together.

Ryan pulled on a pair of boxers and rubbed his chest as he made his way out of his room and across the wide hallway. He listened for a moment, but didn't hear anything. He tapped the back of his knuckles on the door.

"Morgan."

Silence. He tapped again and the door eased open just a bit. He pushed it slightly and peered inside. All he saw was a book lying on the bedside table, her jewelry all displayed on the top of the dresser, and a floral robe draped over the bottom of the bed.

Then he heard it. Humming and water running.

Ryan turned his attention toward the bathroom and debated on leaving or following through. He'd come here for a reason and the apology couldn't wait. She deserved better.

He tapped on the bathroom door and the water and humming instantly ceased.

"Yeah?"

"Thank you for the dinner," he called through the closed door. "I'm sorry about earlier. It was just… I didn't have a great day and I didn't mean to take it out on you."

He waited for a reply, but the door eased open and Morgan stood before him wearing only a towel wrapped around her. She'd piled those red curls up on top of her head and her face was void of any makeup.

She looked like a damn fantasy come to life. Yeah, coming in here had been a mistake. He could have texted or called from across the hall and saved them from this face-to-face meeting. Between them, they only had two scraps of clothing for coverage.

If he slept with her now, she'd think that was all he wanted from her. And while everything in him needed Morgan in his bed, he also had to think long-term. If they didn't get some ground rules set, they'd never accomplish a joint union that served both of them and their child.

"You're entitled to bad days," she told him. "Don't worry about apologizing to me."

He never wanted to admit she was right, but in this instance, she was. Bad days were simply part of life and the fact that she understood churned a deeper emotion within him that he wasn't quite ready to face.

"Did you eat dinner?" he asked, turning away from any unwanted thoughts.

"I had some, but decided a relaxing bath sounded better."

He couldn't stop his eyes from traveling over all of that creamy exposed skin. He clenched his fists at his sides when she eased the door open a bit farther.

"There's plenty of room in here for two," she offered.

Why had he refused this before? Oh, yeah. He was trying to be a gentleman and see if they could make this work if they removed sex from the equation.

That was the most idiotic plan he'd ever had in his life. No man would turn down such an invitation. But, again, she deserved better. She deserved a man who would treat her with respect and he wanted to show her that they should get married. And she wouldn't marry him if all they had was a physical connection.

So no matter how damn much he wanted her, he couldn't have her.

Ryan smoothed a wayward strand of hair from her forehead and trailed his fingertip down her jawline.

"You are too tempting," he murmured. "But I wasn't kidding about not sleeping together. We have to try at something solid that isn't based on the emotions of sex or fighting."

"All we have to do is whatever the hell we want," she retorted. "There's no reason for rules here, Ryan. We both want each other, so why are you doing this?"

He took a step back and crossed his arms over his chest. "Because our baby needs parents that can work together, who might actually have something in common other than chemistry. I want to show you that we can have it all if we try."

"So you don't care that you'll go back to your room and leave me alone and aching? I know you'll be just as miserable. Come in here with me. Let me help you forget about your bad day."

Oh, she could certainly make him forget a good many things. But he had to keep his eye on the main goal and that had to be his family. He had a heritage to protect and plans were already in place. He'd been close once to love and legacy. Then he realized love didn't matter, but family meant everything. He yearned to find that again and refused to ever give up. Now that he had a second chance, he would fight with everything in him to secure the future of Yellow Rose.

"When you decide to marry me, you'll be in my bed."

Ryan turned and left her room before he betrayed the vow he made to himself. He wanted the hell out of her and she knew it. She had a valid point that they were alone and nobody was there to stop them. He completely understood and agreed. But he needed her to see where he was coming from and until that moment came, Ryan would have to stand his ground.

Ten

Ryan had just stepped out the door to head to the stables when a familiar SUV pulled up to the house. He made his way to the drive that separated the house from the path to the main stable as Jayden stepped from his vehicle.

"Hey, man. What are you doing out this way?"

Jayden adjusted his sunglasses and stopped at the edge of the yard. "Had to run some errands for Zanai and was going by. Just thought I'd stop and see why I haven't heard from you in over a week."

Ryan really didn't know where to start with his friend, but he did know he shouldn't share everything. Not quite yet.

"I'm sorry," Ryan told him. "I meant to get back

with you yesterday, but then we had a stillborn foal and the entire day went to hell."

"Hate to hear that. Is there anything you need?"

Ryan shook his head. "We're all good here."

"Well, the main reason I wanted to talk was to tell you Zanai and I are getting married."

Ryan smiled. "Congratulations. When is the day?"

"We're looking at spring. Zanai is in a hurry, but she wants better weather. I really don't care when we do it, so long as she knows she's mine forever."

Forever. That was what marriage was all about. Not love or feelings or all of those up and down emotions. Ryan wanted this family and he wanted his own forever. He longed for a stable, secure relationship for himself and his child. Those things were far more important than love.

"I'm there," Ryan assured him. "Can you stick around? Maybe come in and have a drink? This is worth celebrating."

Jayden shrugged. "If you have the time, but I don't want to intrude."

Ryan slapped his friend on the back and gestured toward the house. "Come on in. I've got a twenty-year bourbon I've been saving for a celebration."

"You don't want to save it for your own celebration?" Jayden asked as they reached the door.

"Don't worry, I have plenty of other bottles."

As soon as they stepped inside, Jayden started laughing.

"Since when did you become so festive?" he asked.

Jayden turned and his eyes landed right on a pair of cowgirl boots by the front door.

"And since when did you wear a tiny boot?"

Jayden's eyes came up to meet Ryan's and he realized his mistake. Ryan should have offered anything else other than coming inside.

"No wonder you couldn't return my calls or texts." Jayden rested his hands on his hips and raised his brows. "Well, who is she? The same woman who caught your eye at the Masquerade Ball?"

No need to lie about the woman in his life, especially since most of the town saw him and Morgan leaving that party together. That didn't mean he had to go into the whole baby situation, though. Some things were still too fragile to discuss and Ryan still struggled to grasp that hard nugget of reality, as well.

"Yes, it's Morgan."

Jayden stared for another minute before a bark of laughter echoed in the foyer.

"I should have known. Man, you two work fast. We just had the Masquerade Ball a month ago. You went from dancing and kissing to living together? No wonder you didn't want to give me relationship advice when I asked you weeks ago."

Yeah, well, Ryan still was in no position to discuss relationships or dole out any advice on the topic.

"So, you're serious?" Jayden asked. "I never thought I'd see the day you finally settle down. After Margie—"

Ryan held up a hand. "She's long gone and I'm in a good place."

Physically, not emotionally…or sexually.

"Well, I'm glad you found a way to move on and Morgan is one beautiful woman. You two look good together."

Ryan motioned toward the front living area. "Come on in and have a seat. Let's talk about anything but relationships."

Jayden settled into a leather club chair as Ryan pulled out the bourbon and two Glencairn glasses from the mini bar in the corner of the room.

"Want to discuss Heath putting my family through the wringer or the fact that old survey says oil isn't there and yet he's still not backing down?"

"I'm not surprised." Ryan took the glasses and headed to take a seat across from Jayden. "He believes your families have something that belongs to him. And there's no dodging the guy. His brother is marrying Morgan's sister in a couple weeks. Those two have started mending whatever fences they've torn."

Ryan set the glasses on the round table between them and eased back in his seat. Everyone in town seemed shocked that Heath was persisting. Most people had assumed that once the old surveyor's report turned up in the investigation, Heath would give up. But instead he'd hired his own surveyor. Ryan honestly didn't want to get caught up in the chaos considering he had his own issues to deal with.

Complete the survey below and return it today to receive up to 4 FREE BOOKS and FREE GIFTS guaranteed!

FREE BOOKS GIVEAWAY
Reader Survey

1
Do you prefer stories with happy endings?

◯ YES　　◯ NO

2
Do you share your favorite books with friends?

◯ YES　　◯ NO

3
Do you often choose to read instead of watching TV?

◯ YES　　◯ NO

YES! Please send me my Free Rewards, consisting of **2 Free Books from each series I select** and **Free Mystery Gifts**. I understand that I am under no obligation to buy anything, no purchase necessary see terms and conditions for details.

❏ **Harlequin Desire®** (225/326 HDL GRK3)
❏ **Harlequin Presents®** Larger-Print (176/376 HDL GRK3)
❏ **Try Both** (225/326 & 176/376 HDL GRLF)

FIRST NAME

LAST NAME

ADDRESS

APT.#

CITY

STATE/PROV.

ZIP/POSTAL CODE

EMAIL ❏ Please check this box if you would like to receive newsletters and promotional emails from Harlequin Enterprises ULC and its affiliates. You can unsubscribe anytime.

Your Privacy – Your information is being collected by Harlequin Enterprises ULC, operating as Harlequin Reader Service. For a complete summary of the information we collect, how we use this information and to whom it is disclosed, please visit our privacy notice located at https://corporate.harlequin.com/privacy-notice. From time to time we may also exchange your personal information with reputable third parties. If you wish to opt out of this sharing of your personal information, please visit www.readerservice.com/consumerschoice or call 1-800-873-8635. **Notice to California Residents** – Under California law, you have specific rights to control and access your data. For more information on these rights and how to exercise them, visit https://corporate.harlequin.com/california-privacy.　　HD/HP-122-FBG22_HD-HP-122-FBGVR

"Chelsea's wedding is going to be awkward as hell." Jayden picked up his glass and swirled the contents. He took a sip of his bourbon, then another. "Damn. That's good. I'm glad I stopped by."

Ryan laughed and tipped his glass up in a mock cheers. "You're always welcome here, my friend."

Jayden relaxed into his seat and rested his elbow on the arm. "So, let's get back to Morgan."

Ryan knew Jayden wouldn't let this topic go. But some things had to be kept private and everything going on between him and Morgan was best left between them.

"How about we discuss the bachelor party?" Ryan suggested. "Vic and I will make sure you have the bourbon you want."

Jayden nodded and just like that, the conversation shifted and the weight lifted from Ryan. He knew it was only a matter of time before everyone knew just how serious he and Morgan had become. They couldn't hide forever.

Morgan pulled into the drive and waited for the gate to slide open. She still wasn't used to coming here after work. She had never lived with a man outside of her own family before. This unique situation was certainly not one she'd ever planned on, but she'd told her parents the truth and they fully supported her decision to stay with Ryan.

Pregnant from a one-night stand, living with a man she barely knew, and trying to keep a secret from the town seemed like just the gossip she never wanted to be a part of. Yet here she was.

Part of Morgan thought she'd miss the home she grew up in, but she couldn't deny how much she loved her room and the little touches Ryan had added to make her feel special. Fresh flowers each day really went a long way to making her feel more at ease. She couldn't be bought into a marriage, but she wasn't going to turn down being wooed.

Wooed? Did that word seriously just roll through her mind? Clearly she needed more sleep or something. None of this was about romance. Even Ryan would agree to that. Neither of them cared about love or any other deeply binding emotion. She wasn't sure of his backstory or what made him so adamant on marriage, but whatever happened in his past had nothing to do with her or what was happening now.

As she approached the house, she stopped her car and just stared at the sight ahead of her. Then she laughed. This man was confusing the hell out of her with his opposing views on the holiday.

Morgan pulled on up and killed the engine. She grabbed her bag and stepped from the car.

"Now you decide to do exterior lights?" she called out.

Ryan glanced down from his position on the ladder. "You wanted lights. Here you go."

"I would have helped you had you waited until I got here."

She almost said *home*, but this wasn't her home. This was only a temporary arrangement.

"And I'm sure you have guys who would have done this," she added.

Ryan hooked the last bit of the strand in the fastener and started to climb down. He wiped his hands on his jeans as he took a step back to survey his work.

"I'm sure I do, but I'm also capable. I had to go into town and buy the damn things so I hope this is what you like."

Even in his growling, Morgan knew he'd done all of this because he cared. But how deep did that care run?

Yes, they were having a baby together, but she couldn't let that be the only reason she stayed with him. A child was no reason to declare your entire life to one person…who could very well be the wrong person. Caring and loving were two completely different things and one day, he might want to fall in love and do this marriage thing for real.

Morgan crossed the yard and stood beside Ryan. The twinkling white lights across the porches and banisters, combined with the garland and gorgeous wreaths on the windows and doors, brought a tear to her eye.

"It's magical," she murmured. "For someone who doesn't want to go all out, you did just that."

"Carmen at the supply store guided me," he confessed. "She's been here before so she told me exactly what I should do and I bought everything she said because I didn't want to screw this up."

And that statement right there tugged at Morgan's heart in a way she'd never known possible. He must have spent the entire day doing this for her after going through such a bad day on the ranch yesterday. He'd turned right around and put her wants ahead of his healing.

Morgan turned to face him and rested her hands on his shoulders.

"Thank you."

Ryan reached up, swiping a tear from her cheek. "Are those good tears? I never can tell when women cry."

"Definitely good tears." She wrapped her arms around him and held tight. "This was the best surprise. I don't know the last time anyone surprised me."

Ryan's strong arms came around her and Morgan closed her eyes, wanting to lock this moment in her core memory forever. Ryan was more than a wealthy rancher or good-time guy. He had a giving heart, which made his mood yesterday all the more concerning.

Not only that—to experience this side of Ryan really tugged at something internally for her. How could he be even more tempting than before? Seeing him go out of his way with such a sweet gesture only added another layer of temptation she didn't know if she could resist.

Morgan eased back and held his face in her hands.

The coarse hair from his beard tickled her palms, but she was finding that she loved the tickling sensation.

"What happened yesterday?" she asked. "And don't blow me off."

Ryan's lips thinned and he reached out, curling his fingers around her wrists as if holding on for support.

"We lost our foal." He blew out a sigh and added, "We tried everything and I had our vet there, too. Nothing we did could save her."

Morgan knew that ache of losing an animal. Ranches were full of so many, but losing even one was a painful experience.

"I'm really sorry," she told him. "I know that doesn't change the situation. Even though I gave up ranch life, I still grew up on one and I understand what you're going through. I remember the first animal we lost when I was little."

Morgan turned her hands and held on to his between their bodies as she recalled the memory.

"Dad wanted all the kids in the barn to watch the birth because he was determined that we saw everything, good or bad, at the ranch. We had no idea the calf would be stillborn. Honestly, maybe that's what turned me off to that lifestyle. I was only eight, but I remember thinking I didn't like pain and I didn't like the darkness that seemed to overshadow us that day. I only wanted to see the good and the pretty of the world."

Ryan's soft smile had her heart doing a flip. "And here you are making the world, or at least Royal, beautiful."

Morgan's breath caught in her throat. She hadn't thought of her life that way. She just knew she loved fashion and she had a smart business sense about her. You couldn't grow up on a successful ranch and not be business savvy. But she'd never put all of that together until just this moment.

"Do these decorations make you want to marry me?" he asked.

Morgan tried not to cringe because even though he offered her a grin, she knew he wasn't entirely joking.

"Not even going all out on Christmas decorations will make me marry you," she informed him. "But you did earn yourself an invite into my bed."

Ryan released her and shook his head. "I'm pretty sure you would have let me in there no matter what."

"True," she agreed. "But now I'll let you have all the control. I could just…you know, lay there and let you have your way with me."

Ryan's eyes closed and he rested his forehead against hers. "You could tempt a saint, I swear."

"Is that a yes?" Morgan slid her arms around his waist. "You don't have to be noble on my account."

He chuckled and shifted to look her in the eye. "Oh, I'm not noble. I'm just planning for the future and what's best for this family. Say yes to marriage and I'll let *you* have control in the bedroom."

She didn't want control enough to give up her freedom or to be trapped. Morgan stepped away and adjusted her purse strap on her shoulder.

"I guess we'll both just have to stay in control outside of the bedroom."

Which was a shame when they were both so, so good inside.

Eleven

Ryan stared at the black-and-white image. He'd seen plenty of livestock ultrasounds, but he had no clue how the hell to decipher anything with Morgan's. The doctor assured them this little peanut shape was indeed their baby. A strong heartbeat and measuring right on target eased a worry he hadn't realized he'd been holding on to.

The first baby picture of his child. He really didn't know where to put it because nobody could see this. He'd have to keep it in his bedroom because anywhere else in the house he would run the risk of one of his staff seeing it.

He hated hiding the pregnancy like something to be ashamed of. Nothing about what he and Morgan shared should be labeled as shameful, but he also had to respect her wishes. She wanted to share the news at the right time. Her family knew but were sworn to secrecy. He hoped they could share an engagement announcement at the same time.

Ryan stepped from his truck and headed into the house. He knew exactly where he'd keep the ultrasound photo...right next to the ring he'd purchased the day after he had discovered the pregnancy.

He and Morgan had parted ways after the doctor's appointment this morning. He had paid a hefty sum for a private appointment at a discreet office two towns over with the doctor Morgan wanted. If they were keeping this under wraps for now, they couldn't exactly be seen together at the ob-gyn's office in Royal.

Ryan had been relieved to know the baby and Morgan both looked great and the summer due date would be here before he knew it. He needed to bring in a designer to work with Morgan on the nursery. No doubt she would want her touch on everything and he would give her nothing but the best.

She might see his move as over-the-top, but his child and the woman he planned on marrying would both have the best. And even though Morgan could buy anything she wanted, he still planned on keeping her satisfied, with no need to worry about a thing.

Maybe she would see that he wasn't trying to buy her. Moving in for this short time would show her just how genuine he truly was and how serious he took family matters. Having lost both of his parents when he'd been in his early twenties and then having a fiancée walk out on him days before their wedding, Ryan wanted to cling to the hope that this time he would have his own family. This time Yellow Rose would have a future with the next generation. He didn't start anything this grand just to grow old alone and sell to the highest bidder. Everything he did, he did with the intention of growth and legacy.

There were several things he needed to get done on the ranch, but he also had a few things to do before Morgan returned home after work.

Home. He kept thinking of his place as her home, but she only occupied one little corner of his three-story house. Oddly enough, he wanted her to put her stamp on other areas. Maybe she'd leave her purse on the kitchen island or a blanket on the sofa where she'd been watching a movie.

Even seeing another set of dishes in the sink would make him so happy. He shouldn't be this excited, but damn it, he'd accomplished all he'd wanted as far as his career. Now it was time to focus on building his family and settling them here at Yellow Rose Ranch.

Once Ryan had the photo locked away in his bedroom, he changed into his work boots and headed down to the stables. He pulled his cell from his pocket and made a few calls to put his plan into motion. Everything had to be perfect.

He would win her over…and he'd win this challenge.

* * *

The day had been busy and long, which only led to the Rancher's Daughter being extremely profitable.

As much as Morgan loved her business and providing for her customers, everything in her body ached. She hadn't expected pregnancy to shrink her energy levels, but since she was brand-new at all of this, she was learning day by day.

Kylie had opened the store this morning, then left around one. Morgan seriously didn't think she could have gotten through the day without her, but she still needed to hire another employee. Sooner rather than later.

All Morgan wanted was to soak in a hot bath and to lie in bed and read. Kylie planned on opening again tomorrow, which meant Morgan could hopefully sleep in a little.

Or if she had her way, she'd be lying in bed with Ryan, but he still had a roadblock put up. She had every intention of wearing him down…but maybe tonight wasn't the time. Tired didn't even begin to describe her body. She should be thankful, though. She still didn't have any morning sickness.

Morgan stepped into the house and the aroma of garlic and yeast instantly filled her senses. She followed the smell into the kitchen where Ryan stood at the island dishing up dinner.

"I heard lasagna was your favorite."

Morgan stilled. How on earth had he heard that? Had Vic called and spoken to Ryan?

He turned from the island and faced her. His hands dropped to his sides and he closed the distance between them. Morgan held her breath as he reached out and tipped her chin up.

"You're working too much. Let Kylie take on more or hire someone else before you wear yourself down."

"I'm working like I always do."

His fingertips feathered across her jawline until he cupped her cheek. She resisted the urge to turn in to his comforting touch.

"You're a different person than you were six weeks ago," he reminded her. "The doctor said you'd get tired easily and to listen to your body."

Morgan laughed. "Right now my body is saying it just wants to relax in a bubble bath, but that dinner smells amazing."

"Go on upstairs and relax. Dinner isn't going anywhere."

She wrinkled her nose and glanced over his shoulder. "It looks like you went to a lot of trouble."

"Nelson did everything," he replied. "All I did was keep it warm. Go on. Eat when you're ready."

Morgan hesitated, but she really just wanted out of this bra and off her feet. She had no idea her breasts would be the first thing to change. Her bra was already getting a little too tight for her comfort. How would she be in another month? Another six months?

She also hadn't realized just how much she could change in a month. Never did she think she'd be living in Ryan Carter's home—even if temporarily. Then again, he'd changed so much, as well. Or maybe he'd been the same and she just now realized what a good heart he'd been hiding.

Either way, all of this confusion stirred a deeper emotion within her. She had to hold her ground, though. Everything had been moving so fast and her thoughts bounced between confusion and excitement.

Morgan made her way up to her room and as soon as she crossed the threshold and flicked the light on, she gasped.

There in the opposite corner right next to the double doors leading out onto her own private balcony stood a Christmas tree at least six feet tall, completely adorned with clear lights, white-and-gold ornaments that glistened in the light, and a gorgeous angel tree topper.

Morgan stood frozen, simply taking in the sight before her. If Ryan was trying to play some kind of game with her emotions, he was doing a damn good job. Tears pricked her eyes and she really wished these pregnancy hormones would calm down.

She closed the door behind her and stripped out of her clothes. After running a warm bubble bath, she nearly cried as she sank into the bliss.

This was all she'd dreamed of all day long. Her own en suite bathroom was pretty grand, but she didn't have a large soaker tub like this. Her mother loved to redecorate, perhaps she could help. A complete bathroom overhaul wasn't a bad idea.

When her belly growled, Morgan figured she'd been in the tub long enough. The water had started to cool and she really did need to eat. Then she'd be ready to lie in bed and just relax. She'd likely fall asleep the moment her head hit the pillow even though it was still early in the evening.

Morgan grabbed the towel from the warming bar and dried off before wrapping herself up in the oversized terry cloth. Even these towels were amazing. How did a bachelor have all the right things that any woman would love?

No, not any woman. He wanted her. Not for love, but out of obligation and some sense of loyalty. If she wasn't pregnant, Morgan knew she wouldn't be here right now. And the idea of another woman in her place sent an instant burst of jealousy through her.

Why would she care who Ryan married or moved in after this month was up? She didn't want any part of a relationship her brother hatched by some silly trick. How could she trust such a connection that stemmed from a one-night stand?

Her siblings were all married or getting married to people they absolutely loved, and that was great for them, but Morgan was just fine being single or dating.

Honestly, though, she couldn't think of the last date she'd been on and once the baby came, she had a feeling her social life would only consist of mommy-and-me playdates.

Even then, Morgan didn't like the idea of another woman sharing Ryan's bed, learning his touch, knowing what made him irritated or sad or angry. Morgan had learned many of his character traits and for reasons she couldn't explain, she wanted to hold every bit of that information close to her chest and keep it all for herself.

She padded barefoot into the adjoining bedroom to grab her robe off the end of the bed. Again, she stopped. Now there was a tray of food on the table beside her bed. She moved closer and smiled at the hearty portion of lasagna, bread, salad and tea. On the perfectly folded napkin was an assortment of colorful vitamins.

The handwritten note simply said, *For you and the baby.*

She'd been taking her prenatal vitamins with each meal and clearly Ryan had been paying attention. How much had he taken in? Clearly her love for the holidays and the time she got off work he'd noticed.

She also couldn't help but wonder if he was caring for her to persuade her into marriage or if he would be doing all of this stuff anyway had she already agreed.

Regardless, she was thankful and she'd tell him just how much. Of course, she'd rather show him, but he was still being difficult.

Morgan slid on her robe and tightened the belt, wondering how she could spin all of this to her advantage. Perhaps she could start persuading him. She hadn't tried enough seducing because she'd been so tired lately, but each night she went to bed, knowing he was so close and aching for his touch.

Now that she'd had him, she didn't know how she'd ever turn to anyone else. It would be impossible not to compare other lovers to Ryan.

Since her time was limited here and Ryan was still standing his ground, it was time for her to take charge and go after what she wanted. Isn't that what he was doing?

Ryan Carter had finally met his match…and his ultimate challenge.

Twelve

Ryan rounded the curve of the staircase and headed toward his room. As he started down the hallway, he stilled and his attention landed on Morgan's closed door.

Was she in there right now soaking in a hot bath with iridescent bubbles kissing her skin? She likely had that red hair piled on top of her head. Maybe a few wayward strands had fallen to lie against her neck.

When he'd brought her food up earlier it had taken every bit of his willpower not to go on into that bathroom and help make sure she was good and relaxed.

Ryan cursed beneath his breath. He could still go in there right now and take her. She'd more than shown him that she was willing, but how would that further his goal? He didn't want a temporary fix to any situation. He wanted Morgan forever to help him build the next generation and be one cohesive unit as a family.

Maybe she would come around. He had to keep looking ahead and whether Morgan believed him or not, this decision would be the best for her, too.

He only wished he didn't have to be so damn noble like she'd accused. He'd used every last bit of his self-control where she was concerned. Over the past few nights, he'd lain awake wondering what she was doing across the hall and wondering if she was over there thinking of him, too.

Usually ranch business kept him tossing and turning, but now the insomnia could only be attributed to the fiery beauty who'd turned his world upside down, yet still refused his proposal.

Ryan ignored the invisible tug toward her room and cursed himself once again as he headed to his. He had some emails to look over and some decisions to make regarding the sale of several head of cattle and he wanted to explore adding in more mares. There was a new ranch about an hour away that he hoped to do business with and build a solid relationship with the new owner.

A nice glass of bourbon and a night on the balcony doing some work should help take his mind off Morgan. Probably not, but he had to at least try and he still had this business to run.

Ryan stepped into his room and closed the door,

immediately pulling his tee over his head. He toed off his boots and removed his socks. Decompressing and forcing himself to relax was the only way he was going to get through these next few weeks.

Ryan went to the dry bar in the living area of his room and poured three fingers of his favorite bourbon. He pulled his cell from his pocket and opened up the emails as he headed toward the double doors leading to his balcony. Maybe a little fresh air would calm him.

He loved the outdoors and he loved the vantage point that his room provided over the property. He could see the barns, the pond, and some of the acreage with his livestock dotting the horizon.

There was nothing he loved more than seeing what he'd created. Knowing now that he had an heir to pass his estate to warmed and settled something deep inside. He'd been given a second chance with the most unexpected woman. They would make a dynasty together, of that he was sure. He was pretty damn proud of what he had to offer to not only Morgan, but their baby.

He'd taken wise investments and the inheritance from his parents and turned everything into the Yellow Rose Ranch. No other name would have fit this place. His mother had a plethora of yellow roses in her gardens year after year and he always wanted to remember her. The homage only seemed fitting.

The moment he stepped onto his balcony, Ryan stilled.

"Thank you for the dinner and the Christmas tree."

Morgan sat on the sofa against the solid balcony wall with her bare legs stretched out along the cushions. Her hair was piled on top of her head as he'd imagined…and that damn robe splayed open giving him the best view he'd ever seen on this balcony. The only thing beneath the parted material was moonlit skin.

Damn. She was good at this.

"You're welcome."

Everything in him had to tear his gaze away from all of that exposed skin that he desperately wanted to touch. His grasp on this invisible string was about to snap and he didn't know how much longer it would hold.

"Did you not want to sit on your balcony?" he asked. "It has a nice view, too."

A slow grin spread across her face as her gaze dropped to his bare chest. "Not like this."

His body instantly stirred and the loose grip on his resolve was nearly gone.

"You're playing a dangerous game."

Morgan swung those long, lean legs over the side of the couch and came to her feet. She spread her robe even wider as she rested her hands on her hips.

"No, I'm taking what we both want."

And that was it. The gauntlet had been thrown down and he was damn well going to pick it up because there was only so much a man could take.

Ryan crossed to her in two strides.

Without a care or a second thought, he jerked that robe from her shoulders and let it fall to the floor behind her. Her eyes widened as did her smile, as if she knew she had won.

In his defense, though, he sure as hell hadn't lost.

"Finally," she murmured a second before he captured her lips.

Ryan couldn't touch her enough. He wanted his hands all over her. He gripped her backside and pulled her hips flush wish his, her breasts pressed against his bare chest. He was not a damn bit angry that he'd given in.

They both needed this and she was sexy as hell for taking charge.

"Were you coming out here to work?" she muttered against his mouth.

"Work doesn't exist for the moment." He framed her face with his hands and forced her attention on him. "Nothing else matters but right here, right now."

Her eyes remained fixed on his as her hands went to the buckle on his belt. Ryan sucked in a breath as she worked his jeans open and shoved them down, taking his boxer briefs with them.

"I hope your ranch hands are in the bunkhouse." She laughed.

"You ask now after you've already been sitting out here practically naked?"

She shrugged. "I was only worried about you, nothing else."

His heart clenched and he hated that unwanted

sensation. He didn't want his heart involved. He'd tried that before and it had left him emotionally scarred.

This was sex. Just like the other two times with Morgan. There were no deeper feelings to explore.

"They're probably all in the bunkhouse," he assured her. "And it's well on the other side of the barns. Nobody can see what we're doing up here."

She poked a finger into his chest. "Then take a seat, cowboy."

Who was he to ignore a demand like that?

Ryan shifted around her and sank down onto the sofa. Morgan stared down at him. The gentle evening breeze picked up her stray tendrils and sent them dancing about her shoulders. Morgan's body seemed to radiate a shimmering beauty with the moonlight and soft glow spilling out from his bedroom.

She rested a knee on one side of his hips, then straddled him with her other. Delicate hands came to rest on his shoulders as she continued to keep her wide stare on him.

There was more than passion in those expressive eyes, there was determination. He could appreciate her drive and her desire. They were matched in so many ways, yet he couldn't look at this as more than a smart decision to further the future goals of his ranch.

Ryan gripped her hips as she joined their bodies and every thought in his head vanished. There was only now with this woman. Her short nails bit into his skin as she began to move. Her quick actions were a sure sign she'd had too much pent-up passion as he'd held her off as long as he could. He should have known he wouldn't be able to last the entire month without having her and he should have known Morgan would go after what she wanted.

Knowing she was this turned on, this aroused for him, only added to his pressing need for her. Ryan gripped her backside with one hand and thrust the other up into her hair, sending the knot tumbling down. Vibrant red strands fell around her shoulders as she dropped her head back and arched into his body.

Her hips jerked faster and watching her lose herself in the intensity of the moment was all he needed to let go. They'd been dancing around this moment for days and he couldn't hold back any longer.

Ryan pulled her mouth to his and captured her lips. He needed to feel all of her, to touch her any way and every way he could. Morgan's body calmed seconds before his and Ryan banded his arms around her waist. He nipped at her lips gently before easing back and staring up at her.

Those full, damp lips, her hair in a mass all around them, and those sexy heavy lids with her eyes locked onto his had Ryan already positive this was just the start of tonight's festivities.

"Thanks for the tree and dinner," she told him with a smile.

"You already told me that."

He smoothed the hair back from her face, wanting to see more of her and wondering if he'd ever get enough.

"I wanted to thank you properly," she amended.

Ryan ran his hands up and down that smooth skin on her back and down over her hips. She shivered beneath his touch, which only proved to him he held some power over her. She wasn't immune to his advances or uncaring. She wanted this, maybe from a different standpoint than him, but didn't they technically have the same goal in mind?

They both wanted stability for their child and they both had amazing chemistry. Why couldn't she see this was so much more than temporary or some challenge to see who could win? They both could.

Soon she would come to realize that this might not be the same type of relationship as so many in Royal had found with everlasting love, but he and Morgan had a pretty damn good possibility to be a dynamic couple. Love didn't have to factor in one bit.

When she trembled once again, Ryan gathered her close and came to his feet, with her still wrapped all around him.

"It's a little chilly out here." He kept his focus over her shoulder as he carefully carried her back into his room. "Maybe you can keep expressing your thanks in here where it's warmer and more comfortable."

Her lips grazed his neck. "I still have plenty of ways to show my appreciation."

Ryan's entire body heated up all over again at her sultry tone and promise. He hoped like hell this was just one of the many nights she would spend in his bed and wondered if they were just one step closer to putting that ring on her finger.

Thirteen

"I told Vic and Chelsea they could tell Aubrey and Nolan about the baby. And Layla could tell Josh."

Morgan waited for Ryan to say something, but he just tightened his hold around her as she leaned into his side. They'd gathered blankets and come back out to the balcony to enjoy the beautiful night sky. Ryan had lit the heater and they lay entangled on the sofa. Clothes were still strewn about, but she was in absolutely no hurry to pick them up.

She'd come home with every intention of going to bed early, but relaxing with Ryan trumped any book or a nap.

The clear sky gave them a spectacular unobstructed view of the stars and full moon. The magical night enveloped her, giving her a glimpse of too many possibilities. But she couldn't let her imagination get away from her. She couldn't allow herself to feel too much or to give her heart an opportunity to break. She had to focus on their child and not be selfish with looking for anything more than a stable foundation.

"I didn't know we were making an announcement yet."

Morgan pulled in a deep breath. "I didn't think it was fair to ask them to keep secrets from their partners."

His fingertips caressed a pattern up and down her bare arm as she lay against him. She couldn't see his face and she wondered what he was thinking.

"Vic was relieved and asked if he could tell Jayden. But I'd like us to tell Zanai and Jayden together, unless you don't want to?"

"It's fine," he told her. "It's funny, we wouldn't even be here if Vic and Jayden hadn't told me you were attracted to me."

Morgan's breath caught in her throat. A heavy dose of dread settled heavy in her belly.

She flattened her hand against his chest and eased herself up to turn and face him.

"What did you say?"

Ryan stared back, clearly unaware of the turmoil and anger that his words had set into motion.

"At the masquerade party," he clarified. "Vic and Jayden told me that you were attracted to me. I honestly had no idea before that. I thought we just annoyed and tolerated each other because the town is so small, it's impossible to avoid everyone."

How could she be so damn foolish? Her own brother and his best friend had clearly been laughing at her behind her back. And now Vic knew she was pregnant and temporarily living with Ryan. Oh, he must really be loving that.

Morgan came to her feet and untangled herself from the blanket. She'd known her brother filled her in about the little trick on her, but she had no idea they'd done the same to Ryan.

"I cannot believe this," she muttered as she grabbed the first article of clothing she could find.

"What's wrong?" Ryan asked.

She jerked on her robe and knotted the belt. "What's wrong? My brother and Jayden. That's what's wrong. You want to know what they told me?"

Ryan's jaw clenched, and his lips thinned. "Probably not."

"They told *me* that *you* had the hots for *me*." Morgan crossed her arms over her chest and tried to calm down, but she was furious. "What the hell game were they playing?"

Ryan stretched his arm along the back of the sofa and with no readable expression. How could he remain so calm when faced with this ugly truth? Morgan was ready to drive over to Vic's house and punch him in the face. How could she trust him? How could she trust any of this situation when all of it had been based on lies and deceit? And now an innocent baby and real feelings had been tossed into the mix.

"Maybe they were playing Cupid," Ryan offered.

Morgan narrowed her gaze. "I'm not amused and why would two grown men even care? This is ridiculous. Damn it."

Ryan shoved the blanket aside and came to his feet. When he reached for her, she wanted to back away, but none of this was his fault.

"I had no idea they did any of this," he told her, gently squeezing her shoulders. "I'm sure getting worked up isn't good for the baby or your sanity. I'll be angry enough for the both of us and talk to Jayden. What the hell had those two been thinking?"

"I just don't get it." She shook her head, trying to make sense of it all. "Vic surely couldn't care less who I end up with as long as I'm happy. I don't understand why he and Jayden said anything at all."

"Who knows? Maybe because they're both in committed relationships and happy and want the same for us."

It still sounded so odd for Vic to meddle like that. Though joking and pranks had always been his style. But hadn't this gone a bit too far? Granted, they'd likely had no idea she and Ryan would tumble into bed that same night.

"I hate being made to seem like a fool," she muttered.

Ryan framed her face and tipped her head up so she had nowhere to look but at him.

"You're not a fool," he corrected her. "And would you honestly take back what happened? We're having a child and you're living here now. I have zero regrets."

Another ribbon of frustration curled through her. She didn't want to give Ryan the wrong impression. She still had no intention of marriage.

"I don't regret the baby," she admitted. "And I'm only here temporarily. I can't—"

Ryan captured her lips and threaded his hands through her hair as he pulled her body flush with his. All thoughts vanished from her mind and she couldn't even remember the point she was trying to make.

When he touched her, he made all of her emotions rise higher than her thoughts. Making her feel more amazing than she ever had seemed to be one of Ryan Carter's many talents.

"Not tonight," he murmured against her lips as he rested his forehead against hers. "No more talking of the future tonight."

At some point they would have to talk, but right now, she just wanted more of his touch. She slid the robe back off and let it slide silently to the floor.

Ryan lifted her and carried her back into his bedroom. She'd never had any intention of sleeping in here with him, but one night wouldn't hurt. She wanted this man and she wanted him to continue to show her just how much he needed her. Because deep down…she needed him, too.

* * *

"Why did you have to call us in here so early?" Vic asked.

Morgan had asked Vic, Chelsea and Layla to her store before she opened. She needed to talk to them privately and this was the only place that would ensure they wouldn't be overheard.

Morgan stared at her brother and sisters and tried to find the right words because the more she had thought about what Vic and Jayden did, the angrier she became. Her sisters likely didn't know any of this had taken place, but since they knew the rest of the secret, it was only right to have them here now.

Vic didn't look a bit relaxed as he stood beside the plush white high-back chair where Chelsea sat. He had his hands propped on his hips with an intense stare aimed directly at her.

"Is something wrong with the baby?" Layla asked.

Her sisters' worried looks had Morgan shaking her head.

"No. The baby is fine and I appreciate you all keeping that secret for now."

"Then what's the problem?" Vic asked.

Morgan rested her hip against the table that had a beautiful display of fluffy throws and fuzzy socks. Her cozy collection had been selling even better than expected for the holidays, which made that risk a success. She only hoped her new maternity line would be as successful.

"Well, dear brother, the problem is you meddling

in my affairs." Morgan laced her fingers in front of her and never wavered her gaze. "How dare you. I trusted you to be there for me in everything in life, not push yourself into molding the outcome."

Layla held up her hands. "Hold up. Care to fill me in?"

"Go ahead," Morgan told Vic. "Let her know what you and Jayden did. I'm sure you found it hilarious at the time yet you look a little nervous now."

Vic adjusted his Stetson and blew out a sigh. "Morgan, we never meant to be deceitful and we sure as hell weren't laughing at you and Ryan."

Chelsea came to her feet. "Would someone tell me what the hell is going on here?"

"Our brother decided that I needed assistance in my social life," Morgan explained. "He and Jayden told me that Ryan was attracted to me, but they told Ryan I was attracted to him."

Morgan redirected her attention back to her brother. "How long before the Masquerade Ball did you two work on that scheme?"

"There was no scheme," Vic explained. "Jayden and I actually thought you and Ryan needed a nudge. You had danced around each other for months. All that bickering and griping at each other, it was clear you both were attracted."

"I can get my own dates," she countered. "Do you know how humiliating that was to discover?"

Vic took a step forward and reached for her hands. "I never, ever meant for you to be angry or upset and

I sure as hell never thought you were a fool. I thought you liked Ryan and he liked you. It was that simple because neither of you were making a move."

When she looked away, Vic cocked his head to continue to hold her in his sights. "Are you angry with how things turned out? I mean, you're living with the man and having his baby."

"No, I'm not sorry how things turned out," she told Vic, then glanced to her sisters. "And it's temporary. Ryan is insisting I marry him and he wanted to play house for a month to convince me."

Chelsea and Layla both smiled and Morgan jerked her hands from her brother's. She didn't like those similar stares looking back at her. She didn't want them to intrude in her personal business. She just wanted...

Hell. She didn't even know anymore.

Perhaps that was the crux of the entire situation. What had started as a joke had turned her life upside down. Her feelings for Ryan grew stronger each day and she didn't like it. She wanted to be in control of her wants and needs, but she hadn't been in control of anything since that night.

Now Vic was smiling, which also grated on her last nerve.

"Stop looking at me like that when I'm trying to be upset," she scolded.

"We just love you and want you to be as happy as we are," Layla explained. "You deserve to find some-

one to spend your life with and you're already starting a family. It just makes sense."

Yeah, it made sense…if she wanted a relationship
based on a meddling brother and a joke.

"I know you all mean well," she told them. "But
what Ryan and I have and are doing is so far removed from what you guys have with the love you've
found."

Chelsea offered a soft smile. "It doesn't have to be."

They didn't understand, and that was fine. Morgan knew what was and wasn't happening with her
relationship with Ryan. She had everything crystal
clear in her head. It was just those sweet gestures
and their passionate night that had thrown her off.
He was trying to sway her into marrying him, but
why? When they had a good thing going like this,
why muddle it with marriage?

She meant it when she said he might find someone later and actually want a marriage where love
existed. She wouldn't want to go through a divorce
and overturn the life they'd created for their child.
Morgan had been blessed with a solid upbringing and
she would settle for nothing less with her own baby.

"That's all I wanted to say," Morgan told her siblings. "I only called Chelsea and Layla in here because
they knew about the baby and I wanted them to know
how all this happened."

"No need to pull in the big guns," Vic said, laughing as he looked at the three sisters. "I'm truly sorry,
Morgan, if you think I was being deceptive, but my

actions were all out of love." Vic wrapped his arms around her and held her tight. "I'd do anything for my little sister."

Morgan laughed. "Well, lay low for a while because I've had about all I can handle of your interference."

Vic laughed and pulled back. "I promise to control myself from here on out, but I'm not sorry I helped you two along. I'm going to be an uncle and spoil this baby."

"I might have already placed a substantial order for baby clothes." Chelsea cringed and shrugged. "I'm not even sorry about it."

"I don't even know if I'm having a boy or a girl." Morgan chuckled.

"Oh, don't worry," Layla assured her. "She ordered plenty of both."

Morgan groaned. She couldn't even imagine the love and gifts that would be poured upon her child. Her family loved big and no doubt they would not hold back here.

"I'm surprised you haven't planned the baby shower," Morgan joked.

"We've booked the TCC already for April and said we were having a girls' night out party so nobody was suspicious. Hope that works for you and Ryan."

Morgan rubbed her head and Vic simply patted her shoulder.

"I'm done intervening, but maybe you were talking to the wrong siblings."

Morgan didn't care if her sisters wanted to throw a

lavish baby shower. Her siblings wanted nothing but the best. She understood that even if she didn't like Vic's course of action.

Ryan wanted nothing but the best for her, too. She only wished her heart wasn't getting involved.

Fourteen

Ryan didn't know if this plan was going to backfire or win him more points, but he hadn't gotten this far in life without taking risks.

His staff was all too thrilled he'd dismissed them for the day when there was still daylight. But Ryan wanted his land to be all about him and Morgan for the day. He wasn't sure when his feelings shifted from wanting to fulfill a legacy to wanting to share all of this with Morgan. No matter when the slow fade happened, Ryan knew without a doubt this was where Morgan belonged. And for her to understand and see that as well, she needed to know about his life and what led him to this point.

There was nothing Ryan was more proud of than

Yellow Rose Ranch. He didn't think that made him shallow or egotistical at all. He'd worked damn hard from his inheritance and wise investments, coupled with smart business sense, and he wanted to show off what he had created.

"What are we doing in the stables?"

Ryan turned as Morgan stepped inside. Her polished look never failed to impress and amaze him. She was everything he wasn't, and she didn't seem to mind that he lived in the same style of clothes every single day. She, on the other hand, never wore the same thing twice.

Today she had on a long black dress, cowgirl boots, and a fitted denim jacket. She could go from the girl next door to the elegant partygoer to the bedroom vixen in a blink and he was quickly discovering just how much he enjoyed each of Morgan's personalities.

"I thought I'd show you around," he told her.

She stopped at the stall that just so happened to house his stallion. Morgan smiled and reached her hand in. Midnight's nose came out enough for Ryan to see. Morgan's gentle touch and kind smile hit him in the gut and all he could think of was how she belonged here. This is where he would raise his family, and his wife would make this ranch her own.

"He's gorgeous." Morgan's hand rested on the side of Max's face as she glanced Ryan's way. "So gentle and sweet."

"He can ride faster than lightning," Ryan added.

"He's my best buddy here and I wouldn't get anything done without him."

She dropped her hand and started moving toward him once again. Those eyes were fixed on his and he still couldn't figure out how she held such a strong power over him. She was absolutely mesmerizing in the most intriguing way.

"And is that why you brought me here?" she asked. "To introduce me to your horse? That's a big step in a relationship."

Ryan couldn't help but laugh. "That's part of the reason. I want to show you around the ranch and since riding a horse is out because of the baby, I thought we'd start here and then we can ride around in the Jeep to look through the acreage."

Morgan reached him and crossed her arms over her chest. "I grew up on a ranch, Ryan. I'm well aware of what they look like and how they work."

"You don't know about Yellow Rose," he corrected her as he turned and held out his elbow. "Walk with me and I'll figure out where to start."

Her eyes darted from his face to his arm and she slid her hand into the crook of his elbow.

"Why don't you start with the name," she suggested. "Yellow Rose Ranch is beautiful, but I do wonder where it came from."

Ryan laid his free hand over hers as they headed toward the other end of the stables. He couldn't recall a time he wanted anything more than to have Morgan agree to marry him. They could live like this together, raise their child and any future children right here. Growing up on a ranch would instill values they wouldn't learn anywhere else.

That was just another area he and Morgan had in common. Even though she'd turned from the life-style, she still knew the ins and outs because she, too, had grown up on a large ranch. This step toward marriage was the right one and the only solution that made any sense. He had to make her see that she wasn't settling, she wasn't losing. In the long run, they'd both be happy.

"My mother's favorite flower was the yellow rose. She always had them in the house and apparently everyone knew because they were all over at her graveside service."

Ryan could finally talk about his mother and re-member the good instead of that instant feeling of pain and loss. Those emotions were still present—they would never go away, but at least he had learned to compartmentalize and he could smile when he thought of her.

"She was always happy, always wanting to make sure everyone around her was in a good mood," he continued. "It's just appropriate that her favorite color was yellow."

"She sounds like an amazing woman."

Ryan nodded as he led Morgan to the Jeep parked behind the stable. "She was, and she would love knowing she'd be a grandmother. No doubt she would have already had a nursery painted and fully stocked. She was all in with everything and loved her family."

"Family is important to both of us."

Morgan started to reach for the handle of the Jeep, but he beat her to it and opened the door. When he gestured her in, she gave him a side-eye and took a seat.

"You know, I'm still moving out at the end of the month, right?" she told him.

Ryan shrugged. "Of course."

He closed the door and rounded the vehicle to climb in behind the wheel. He started up the engine and turned the heat on because even though they were still in Texas, there was a chill in the air in December.

"I own just over twelve thousand acres," he started. "Definitely not the biggest ranch, but I'm proud of it and we're profitable and productive."

Morgan reached over and laid her hand on his on the console. Her soft touch stirred something inside him, something that wasn't arousal...but more pure and innocent. There was almost a comfort and understanding to her gesture.

"This isn't a job interview," she informed him. "Don't sell me this place, Ryan. Why don't you tell me why you love ranch life so much?"

Thoughts instantly swirled around in his head of all the reasons he felt alive on this property. From sunup until sundown, there was so much packed into a day. Not to mention the nostalgia surrounding him at any given time.

"Even on the hardest days, there's nothing else in the world I'd rather be doing."

Morgan squeezed his hand before releasing him. "That's how you know you're in the right profession. Nothing is perfect and it's not always easy, but if you still love your job in those down times, you're blessed."

"It's not just all that I've accomplished here," he added. "I have women and men who work for me that have become like family. This industry forms such strong, tight-knit bonds. Unless you're part of it, the concept is difficult to grasp."

Morgan pointed out her window as he drove along the edge of the pasture.

"What's that peak over there?" she asked.

"That's where we're headed first."

"I'm intrigued." She turned her attention toward him. "I thought we were just coming out here to look at your livestock."

"They're already in another pasture," he informed her. "There's something I wanted you to see other than animals."

Silence settled in the small space as he headed toward the surprise that he hoped didn't backfire. He wanted Morgan to see his life, really see it. She'd turned away from ranching before and here he was trying to pull her back in, to accept this and a marriage that was more like a business arrangement than anything else.

Could he fault her for turning him down?

Even she admitted that she didn't believe in love, so why wouldn't she just give in already?

"I spoke to Vic this morning before the shop opened."

Her statement pulled him from his own thoughts. He already felt sorry for Vic because he knew how angry Morgan had been last night when she'd figured out what had happened.

"How did that go?" he asked.

"I'm still irritated, but I truly think he had good intentions. Even if his methods were ridiculous, he really just wants to see me happy."

"And are you?"

He wanted her to be happy. He hadn't realized how much so, but if she couldn't see herself here or find contentment, then they both lost.

"Morgan—"

"My happiness is the least of my worries."

He reached over and took her hand in his. "Your happiness is equally as important as our child."

"No, it's not."

Ryan maneuvered around the bend as the old structure came into view. Just like every other time he rounded that fence line, memories came flooding back. He hoped they always did because that kept those moments, those people, alive inside him.

"I don't have you at my house just to convince you to marry me," he told her. "I'm trying to do what is best here and I want you to see that you can be happy, *we* can be happy, and that's what will make a good environment for our family. So your happiness is at the top of my priorities."

"How do you do that?" she asked.

"Do what?"

"You make me think and feel and…want."

Her last word came out on a whisper and damn it, he had a burst of hope. Having her come to the decision to stay had been his initial goal. He didn't want to force her to marry him or trick her into this union. Morgan was a strong woman and that was who he wanted by his side raising their child.

Ryan thought it best to say nothing and just let her deal with that statement and her thoughts on her own. His actions would more than show her why he wanted her here.

He pulled up to the old stone house and shut off the engine. He glanced toward Morgan to see her face and gauge her reaction.

"This is an adorable cottage," she stated. "I didn't know this was back here."

"This is where I grew up."

She jerked her attention to him, her eyes wide.

"There was all of this land surrounding the house," he told her. "Some was used for a farm, but it was all owned by different people. I knew I wanted this land, all of it, when I grew up. I wanted to prove I'd made it and that I could do anything I wanted."

Ryan reached up and cupped the side her face. "I know the ranch life isn't for you," he said, stroking his thumb over her bottom lip. "But all I've ever wanted was to be a cowboy, and that little boy's dream came true. I'm not trying to change you into someone you're not, and I'm not asking you to settle or rearrange your life. I'm asking you to be a part of this legacy and just marry me."

Tears filled her eyes and he didn't know if that was the pregnancy hormones or if his words were finally getting to her. All he could offer was his little piece of the world, but never his heart.

"I have another surprise for you after this."

Morgan laughed as a tear slid down her cheek. "Do you sit around and think of ways to keep me guessing what's next?"

Ryan shrugged, swiping away the moisture from her silky skin. "Never thought of it that way. I'm just making sure you know that I'd take care of you and we don't need to get into the fact you're capable of taking care of yourself. I'm well aware. I just want you to know that you'd have a good life here and so would our baby."

He moved his hand to settle over her still flat stomach, all the while keeping his gaze locked on hers.

"I know we would," she admitted as she rested her hand over his. "But everything moved so fast and there hasn't been time to process all the changes so it's impossible to fully grasp another life change."

She closed her eyes and blew out a sigh before meeting his stare once again.

"I see my siblings all falling in love and getting married," she told him. "Part of me wants to believe love is real and if it's real, shouldn't I hold out for that? Shouldn't we both? We deserve to have that person in our lives who will be forever. Because you and I both know that if there hadn't been a pregnancy, then we wouldn't be here right now. There's no love between us, Ryan."

While he did hear what she was saying, and firmly believed that she meant each word, Ryan also knew he was wearing her down. She still had a few more weeks here and he wasn't giving up on his family.

"Not every marriage is a fairy tale." He turned his hand to lace their fingers together. "But we can make our own happy ending."

When she opened her mouth, no doubt to turn him down again, Ryan held up his hand.

"Keep thinking about it," he told her. "Don't turn me down this second. My ego can't take all of the negative answers."

Morgan smiled and that was exactly what he wanted. He didn't want every moment between them to be so intense and serious. He didn't want to fight anymore when they got along so well in too many other areas. The only thing he wanted her to fight for was them. He wouldn't back down, not when he knew Morgan valued family and they had the same ideals.

But he still needed to show her where he came from so she could appreciate what he had now. He loved riding back here and getting the reminder that he'd started from humble beginnings.

Some had questioned why he never tore this place down since it was in the middle of his acreage, but that would be like trying to erase his childhood and those were memories he never wanted to lose.

"I have a few more areas on the ranch I want to show you before head back to the house." He eased away and started the engine back up. "The next surprise is even better than this one."

Morgan chuckled. "Can't wait."

Fifteen

At first, Morgan thought Ryan was just being overly ambitious to get her to marry him, but little by little she realized that beneath their squabbling and butting heads, there was merit. He was a hard worker, something she could appreciate, and he'd done nothing but put her first. Yes, he clearly wanted to cement his legacy, but he'd been working on that all while making sure her needs were not only being met but exceeded.

His old home had been simple and charming, a testament to the humble beginning he'd started with. Each moment she spent with him she realized there were so many layers to this intriguing man. More than she ever thought and she wondered if she'd ever stop discovering more about him.

"Keep your eyes closed."

Morgan stood in the hallway just down from her bedroom with her eyes firmly shut. After she'd seen where Ryan had grown up, he'd taken her to the pond and talked about how he'd teach their child fishing. Then he took her the long way back to the barn and showed her a stall that would house their child's horse when the day came. He had everything all laid out for the future, but right now, he had planned something special.

"They're closed," she insisted. "But I can't stand it. What is the surprise?"

The click of a door echoed in the wide hall, and then Ryan curled his fingers around her arm and started guiding her forward.

"Just walk straight," he advised her. "Almost there and you won't run into anything."

She held out her free hand anyway because she had trust issues. "You're making me nervous."

Ryan's rich laughter filled the space. "Open."

Morgan blinked against the lights as her eyes traveled around the room. She gasped at everything presented before her.

"What have you done?" she asked as she started moving around. She really didn't know what to look at first.

"I hired a designer to come up with some model plans for the nursery," he explained. "I had to keep you out of the house for a bit longer when you got home, so I decided to show you around the ranch."

Morgan turned from the various model displays set up on tables to face Ryan.

"So was that cottage really the house you grew up in?" she asked.

Ryan nodded. "All of that was true and I wanted to show you anyway, so that was the best excuse."

Morgan walked around the model displays, each on their own stand, and was absolutely amazed at what he'd done for her. Never in her life had anyone surprised her to the point she was nearly speechless.

"I don't know what you've thought of for a nursery," he went on. "And whether you live here or not, I still want a place for the baby and I want you to decide what the room looks like. You would have more sense than me about this stuff."

Morgan listened to Ryan as she went back and closely studied the first display. Her heart felt so full, so happy. She really didn't know what to say right now because she was still absorbing the fact Ryan had thought to do all of this on his own. He'd wanted to make a special place for their child and he'd called someone to come up with such intricate plans.

Considering he hadn't known about the baby for too long, he likely had to pay quite a bit for this rush job. But each and every design was so stunning and utterly amazing.

She trailed her finger over the tiny crib, then the model-sized rocker. This was really happening and she bounced from being terrified to being excited. There was no in between.

"I told the designer different styles I thought you liked or information I've taken from your store and the way you dress. You seem to go toward classy with a bit mix of trendy…or that's what the designer said when I described you."

Morgan glanced over her shoulder and smiled. "I can tell you told her something about me. I love them all."

Ryan held his hands out. "Listen, I might wear the same things over and over and I might not know terms or fashion lingo, but that doesn't mean I don't pay attention."

One design had a crisp, clean look to the space with white furniture and pops of green and gold. Very classy. Another design seemed a little more catered to the ranch with the dark woods, deep gray motif. There were a couple for each gender that were clearly for a boy or a girl as well, and Morgan honestly couldn't decide.

"How soon do we need to let her know?" Morgan asked.

Ryan moved to the opposite side of the room where a chaise sat in front of the floor-to-ceiling window overlooking the pond. He rested his hand on the slope of the high back and shrugged.

"I just told her I would be in touch," he replied. "So take your time or make notes about changes you want. She said she could add or remove anything and even combine various aspects from each one. I didn't know if you were thinking something neutral or if you decided to wait to find out the sex. I'm good no matter what, so that's your call."

That familiar, annoying burn started in her throat as her eyes started to fill. Morgan couldn't help but put her head in her hands. She was so tired of these roller-coaster emotions and riding this pregnancy wave. Her thoughts were all over the place from happy to sad to scared to excited. She didn't even know how to feel anymore…not that she could control it anyway.

Ryan was immediately there, pulling her into his warmth and strength.

"Damn it, I knew I overstepped," he murmured. "I'll have her come take everything back and you can design whatever you want. I thought this would be a good thing for you and you might like it, but…"

Morgan shook her head and eased back just enough to rest her hands on his chest and look him in the eye.

"No, this is… Well, this is the greatest surprise I've ever had. You mentioned the sex of the baby and everything just hit me, I guess. I was so shocked when I found out I was expecting and worried about what you would think, what the town would think. I'm fully embracing the reality that our baby is actually coming and we aren't just fodder for the gossip mill."

Ryan smoothed her hair from her face and held her head firmly in his hands as he leaned closer.

"This baby isn't a mistake or gossip," he told her. "We're going to raise her together and she'll have the strength and determination from both of us to do anything she wants in life."

Morgan smiled. "She? You want a girl?"

"I don't care what we have, but I just see you holding a little red-haired beauty. I've had dreams of it, actually."

"Is that so?"

He'd dreamed of their child? He'd dreamed of their baby looking like her, and Morgan couldn't help but wonder if his feelings were going deeper than he cared to admit.

"Are you worried?" she asked.

Ryan slid his hands into her hair and tipped her head back. "Not at all. You and I are going to be great parents."

At least one of them was confident. She used to find his arrogance annoying, but now she found that side of him to be a reassuring quality.

She needed more strength during this time in her life and she found herself drawing from him. Though the ease with which she could lean on him more and more terrified her, if she could keep this relationship physical and superficial, then she could hold on to her heart and not fall for a man who wouldn't love her in return.

Morgan took a step back and pulled her dress over her head. She dropped it to the floor and stood before him wearing only her undergarments and boots.

"You know that very large tub I kept trying to share with you?"

Ryan's mouth quirked as his eyes raked over her body. "I remember."

"Maybe you'll join me?"

She didn't wait for his reply as she walked out of the room. She knew Ryan would follow, and when she heard his boots echoing on that hardwood floor behind her, Morgan smirked all the way into her bathroom.

For now, everything in her world was right...but she'd set the boundaries and all of this was temporary. In just a couple weeks, she'd be back in her home and these passionate nights would just be a memory.

Jonas Shaw, the investigator, had called another important meeting. Morgan had asked Ryan to come with her for support, which really surprised him, but at the same time warmed him. They still weren't ready to come forward with...

What? The baby? Their unsettled living arrangement?

He didn't even know what to call their situation. Likely word had already spread about him being at her shop and the two of them not griping at each other anymore. He wanted to be here for her, in whatever capacity she needed.

The Grandins and the Lattimores all gathered at the Lattimore estate per the private investigator's orders. Jonas only called in both families when he had pertinent information, so Ryan couldn't help but wonder what new development had taken place.

Morgan caught his gaze from across the spacious

formal living area. She'd wanted to stand with her siblings and he didn't want to intrude so he settled in near Jayden.

Yet just that one look she sent him had his heart racing. How did she do that? In a short time, they'd pivoted from verbal sparring to driving each other wild in the bedroom. But there was more…so much more going on between them. Now wasn't time or the place to try to figure out his feelings.

"You have any clue what this would be about?" Ryan whispered to Jayden.

"None," his buddy replied. "But it's got to be major for all of us to be here."

Jonas moved through the room and came to stand in front of the large floor-to-ceiling windows. The tall, slender man had become an ominous staple in Royal since the start of this investigation. He'd been trying to get to the bottom of Heath's claims. Why Cynthia had owned papers saying she'd been gifted untapped oil from Augustus Lattimore and Victor Grandin had remained a mystery.

"I'm glad you all could make it on such short notice," Jonas began as he tapped a folder against his thigh. "As you know, I've conducted several interviews, including ones with Augustus's former secretary, Sylvia Stewart, and the original surveyor, Henry Lawrence. I've also gone through every piece of paper Alexa could find. I now can share my conclusions."

Ryan crossed his arms and waited for the announcement as he glanced around the room to the members of both families, who had been friends for generations. The intermingling of their lives had woven so tightly, Ryan knew no bond could break them. They were all in this together.

"We know Cynthia had a brief relationship with Daniel Grandin," Jonas stated. "Without DNA, it took some time to get proof, but he was indeed Ashley's father."

"It seems that when Victor Sr. discovered the pregnancy, he didn't tell Daniel. He went to his best friend, Augustus. They came up with a plan to offer Cynthia the oil beneath the Grandin estate as a bribe to remain silent. Victor didn't want his son caught up in a scandal. To sweeten the deal, Augustus Lattimore included his land. He couldn't let his best friend's last name be dishonored by his son's meaningless affair."

The gasps around the room seemed to echo, and Nolan reached for Chelsea's hand as her eyes went wide at the revelation.

"So the oil rights weren't an inheritance for Ashley," Nolan chimed in. "They were a payoff to get our mother to keep a dirty secret."

Jonas nodded. "It looks that way. I'm assuming the men figured she wouldn't have the resources to actually claim the oil, so that's when she later married Ladd Thurston. And you all know the rest of that story."

Cynthia had gone on to have the twins, Heath and Nolan.

"So once Heath finds out the rights were meant as a cover-up and not an inheritance, what will he do?" Jonathan Lattimore asked.

All eyes turned to Heath's brother, and Nolan merely shook his head and sighed. "I have no idea, to be honest. He wanted this for our mother, for Ashley. His heart is in the right place. I know not everyone believes that, but he just wants what he thinks belonged to our family."

"I don't even know what to say," Alexa Lattimore finally stated. "This is quite a bit to take in. So, does this end the investigation?"

"Unless I'm needed for more, I believe my part is done," Jonas claimed.

Silence settled over the room and Ryan tried to study each face. The members of these two families might actually have some closure right now, but again, everything hinged on Heath's next move.

"I'm sure this will be all the talk at the Christmas party tomorrow," Zanai whispered to Jayden. "I'll bet Heath doesn't show."

"He doesn't seem like the type of man who would back down or shy away from scandal," Jayden replied.

The Christmas party would certainly be all abuzz with gossip but Ryan had his own worries to deal with…like the fact he was getting deeper with Morgan. Morgan was still hell-bent on leaving his house at the end of the month, but he was just as hell-bent on keeping her there and building a life. He'd been robbed of that before and vowed never again. He needed Morgan to stay.

Because he knew if she walked away from the ranch, she'd never come back.

Sixteen

"You think we can make it out of the house with you looking like that?"

Morgan glanced in the mirror at the reflection of Ryan standing over her shoulder in his bedroom. His eyes held hers and Morgan spun around to take in the full view.

"This is just a white dress." She laughed as she gripped his lapels. "But you in a suit...that's pretty hot."

He started to reach for her, but dropped his hands.

"I don't even know where to touch you without messing anything up."

Morgan took his hands and settled them on her waist. "Never be afraid to touch me," she told him, then tipped her head to the side. "This is the first time I've ever seen you not in jeans and a T-shirt or naked."

Ryan's rich bark of laughter sent a shiver through her.

"Well, I've seen you in all aspects, and this dress is making me want to skip the party completely and see what you have on beneath."

The bundle of nerves that started weeks ago swelled inside her. She had worries, fears and too many unknowns to remain calm.

"I'm wearing your favorite outfit under here."

His lips curved into a sultry grin. "My favorite outfit is nothing."

"Exactly." She patted the side of his face. "There's an excellent liner so you can't see a thing."

Ryan groaned and dug his fingers into her hips as he jerked her even closer. Their hips aligned and there was no mistaking his arousal.

"You're killing me," he growled. "I hate that we're not going together so I can walk in with you on my arm."

"Are you upset that I asked to arrive separately?" she asked, worried she'd put him in an uncomfortable position.

Ryan slid his hands up her arms and held on to her shoulders. "Not at all. I understand we have to find our footing here between us. That doesn't mean I don't want you by my side, but that can wait."

Guilt niggled at her because her feelings were

growing and she had no idea what they were developing into or how to handle all of these sudden life changes. He wanted a marriage based solely on the baby and she couldn't help but feel like something much more was going on between them.

"I never want you to wonder if I think you and this baby are a dirty little secret," she explained. "With my sister's wedding and now this news about Heath and the oil, I don't want to add to all the chatter."

"I get it," he reassured her. "Believe me. After Chelsea and Nolan's wedding, we can figure out the best way to handle everything. People are going to find out about the baby, but maybe they'll also learn there's another wedding happening soon."

Morgan knew he still wanted marriage, now more than ever, and the temptation was so strong. But at the end of the day, she still had to do what she felt was right.

A week ago she was so adamant about saying no and now...well, now her heart told her to go for it, but her head told her to take a step back, evaluate the situation and calm down. Had they moved too fast? Could she trust her emotions at this stage? With so much confusion, she couldn't answer him right now. This wasn't something to rush into or take lightly.

The fact she waffled between her head and her heart really proved the strength of this pull toward Ryan.

"I'm going to head on out," she told him as she

took a step back. "But feel free to peel me out of this when we get back."

The muscle in his jaw clenched as his eyes raked over her once again.

"That's a promise," he assured her. "Now get on out of here before I decide I don't want to wait and I don't care if I mess up your hair and makeup."

Morgan smiled as she grabbed her beaded gold clutch and headed out of her bedroom. The way he looked at her, the things he said to her, the way he treated her…how could she not be falling in love with the man?

Ryan Carter had more power over her than she ever wanted to admit. Love still terrified her, but at the same time, she wasn't sure if that was what she was feeling. All Morgan knew was that she didn't want to settle. That would never change. She only wished she knew more of what Ryan was thinking, of what he was feeling. Did he see her as more than the mother of his child and a bedmate? What held him back from opening up? Fear? Stubborn pride?

There were so many questions that she wouldn't get answered tonight, so she headed to the Cattleman's Club and decided to just have a good time… and she was already anticipating the after-party.

Seeing Ryan across the room proved to be more difficult than Morgan had figured. Actually, she hadn't thought about this part at all. She'd assumed they would arrive separately, be cordial, and maybe even share a dance. But Ryan had barely looked her way and she wasn't quite sure what to think about that.

She also hadn't thought about how odd it would be to walk around without a champagne flute in her hand like everyone else just to blend in. Perhaps she should have some sparkling water.

"You are stunning."

Morgan turned to see Chelsea and Nolan. The two held hands and were both beaming—apparently that was what love did to people. Could she be in love? Was that what had been happening to her over these past few weeks with Ryan? The idea thrilled and terrified her. She didn't know if she could rely on her mixed emotions and land on something so solid and monumental.

"Thank you," Morgan replied. "I see you went with the pale blue dress Good choice."

Chelsea did a mock curtsey. "It was a toss-up when you ordered me three gorgeous gowns. This was Nolan's favorite, so the choice was obvious."

"Before we start mingling and dancing," Nolan chimed in, "I want to address the proverbial elephant that will be in the room tonight."

Morgan turned her attention to Nolan and the poor guy's smile had faltered. Clearly he was embarrassed or uncomfortable at the latest findings, but there was no need to be. Heath was responsible for his own decisions.

"My brother—"

"I already know," Morgan assured him. "There

are no hard feelings from me. Heath wanted to hold on to anything that was your mother's and I can understand that."

Chelsea wrapped an arm around Nolan's waist. The bond these two had was undeniable. They had overcome so many obstacles to be together and Morgan wondered just how they managed to be so strong.

"I feel I should apologize for his actions," Nolan added. "But that's not my place."

"No, it's not," Morgan agreed. "Is he coming tonight?"

Nolan shrugged. "I doubt it. He's pretty angry and frustrated and likely trying to plan his next steps. He wouldn't be in the mood for a party."

Morgan also imagined he wouldn't want to be in a room surrounded by Grandins and Lattimores. Yes, Heath wanted to honor his late mother and sister. It was hard to *completely* fault a guy for defending his mother. Still, he'd angered several people.

But Morgan had her own issues and Heath wasn't one of them right now.

"Nolan, would you care if I stole my sister for just a moment?" she asked. "I promise I won't keep her long."

"Of course."

Nolan kissed Chelsea on the cheek and stepped away, leaving them somewhat alone...save for the other guests mingling. Morgan motioned for Chelsea to follow and led her toward a corner of the room where they could have a little privacy.

"Something wrong?" Chelsea asked. "The baby?"

"No, no. Everything is fine. Well, with the baby. I just… I'm so confused."

Chelsea's brows drew together as she reached for Morgan's hand. "Is it Ryan?"

Morgan chewed the inside of her cheek and nodded. She would not get emotional here. Not only did her makeup look amazing for tonight, she really didn't want to have a meltdown in the middle of a festive holiday party.

"How did you know when you were in love?" Morgan whispered. She was glad she finally had a close relationship with her older sister to be able to ask this.

Chelsea's brows rose and a wide grin spread across her face. "The fact that you're even asking me that gives me so much hope. I love you and Ryan together."

Morgan glanced around to make sure no partygoers were within earshot. From the looks of things, the Royal elite had turned up. Most of the ladies wore dresses that she had ordered through her shop. From golds, to reds, to silvers…there was such a fun variety and they all looked so stunning among the twinkle lights, garlands and rustic lanterns suspended from the ceiling. The entire ballroom had been transformed into a winter wonderland.

"Has he said he loves you?" Chelsea asked.

Morgan shifted her attention back to her sister. "Oh, no. I'm just… I've got these feelings that are all over the place and I can't tell if I just have pregnancy hormones or if there's something more going on. But he opened up about his childhood, drove me around the ranch. He decorated my bedroom with a Christmas tree, and even put up lights and wreaths on his house so I'd feel at home during the holidays."

Chelsea sighed and squeezed Morgan's hands. "Honey, that man has fallen for you. Maybe he's too stubborn to admit it or maybe he hasn't figured it out himself, but that's love. Putting someone else's needs ahead of yours to make sure they are happy is the very definition. Relationships aren't fifty-fifty. They're one hundred-one hundred. Both parties have to put in their full effort for it to work. So if you're having feelings for him, tell him."

The thought of revealing her heart and exposing such a vulnerable piece of herself seemed much more intimate than sex. What if she told him and he didn't feel the same? He still wanted marriage, so what then? She'd still be trapped in a loveless marriage. No, this scenario would be much worse. A one-sided marriage would be a disaster.

"I don't know if I can do it," Morgan admitted.

Her sister released her hands and took a step back. "What? The Morgan I know isn't afraid of anything. You started an upscale boutique in the middle of a town full of ranchers and you've made it one of the most profitable businesses in the area. You're tackling this pregnancy like a champ and you're no-nonsense. So why are you letting your emotions control you?"

Morgan wrinkled her nose. "Because I don't like

failing and I don't like rejection. What can I say? I'm human."

Chelsea's brows rose. "From the way Ryan has been staring this way, I think you might be surprised at his reply when you tell him the truth."

She'd be more surprised if he reciprocated her feelings. Before she said anything, though, she had to make one hundred percent sure she could trust her emotions. She had to be certain because not only did she not want to be hurt, she also didn't want to play with Ryan's heart. He might claim he wasn't looking for love, but what if…

"Thanks," Morgan told her sister. "I don't know what I'm going to do, but I feel better. Now, let's concentrate on your big day. I'm glad it's soon because my boobs are already swelling and I don't know how much longer my dress will fit."

Chelsea rolled her eyes. "You have such problems. You will look gorgeous and if you need the dress adjusted any, I have my seamstress on hand."

Hopefully it wouldn't come to that because Morgan didn't want to have to explain the sudden weight gain.

Her sister gestured with her champagne flute as her focus shifted over Morgan's shoulder. "Looks like your guy is coming this way."

"He's not my guy."

Chelsea merely smirked. Okay, maybe right now Ryan was her guy. She just really wished she knew an actual label to put on this type of unique relationship they had.

"Ladies, you both look beautiful."

Chelsea smiled at Ryan, then glanced to Morgan.

"I appreciate that, though I have a feeling you had already seen my sister before you arrived."

Ryan's naughty grin gave him away and Morgan found her nerves unsettling. How could he do that? A simple smile and the way he could tip his head to one side as if to silently proclaim his innocence took a special skill…and Ryan appeared to have them all. He held so much power over her and he likely had no clue, which was just another reason that exposing her heart could be damaging.

And where would that leave them? They were bound together by a child forever and the last thing Morgan wanted was tension or animosity.

"I'll leave you two alone," Chelsea told them. "I need to find my fiancé."

Once she was gone, Ryan turned toward Morgan.

"Everything okay?" he asked, still keeping his distance.

Morgan forced herself to perk up and be cheerful. She definitely didn't want to start rumors or detract from her sister's big day coming up. Chelsea and Nolan had been through so much to make it to this point and Morgan wanted the entire experience to be absolutely perfect.

"Everything is great," she replied. Then movement just behind Ryan caught her attention. "Oh, there's Vic and Aubrey. I hadn't seen them yet."

"I want a dance with you before the night is over," he told her.

Morgan started to open her mouth, but he held up a hand.

"Nobody will think anything of it after the way we were kissing at the Masquerade Ball. We'll just dance, though. Nothing more, but it will be damn hard to keep my hands in an appropriate position."

There he went again with those sexy words that put instant images inside her mind. She'd only just arrived, but she was already counting down to when they would be back home alone.

Home.

Ryan's place felt like home, but for how long?

Damn it. She was in real trouble here.

Seventeen

Ryan knew Morgan and Chelsea were discussing something serious, likely something to do with him, from the way Chelsea kept glancing his way. He'd love to know what Morgan shared with her sister, but on the other hand, maybe it was best he didn't.

"Aubrey, you look stunning." Morgan reached for her soon-to-be sister-in-law and gave her a hug. "Of course, you always do, but that gold is perfect on you."

"Thank you." Aubrey beamed. "That white with your red hair is drop-dead gorgeous."

Ryan didn't know about color matching and what looked good with skin or hair or any accessories, but he could definitely agree on the drop-dead gorgeous.

Morgan was always a stunner no matter how she dressed, but tonight she absolutely shone.

"What are you getting Chels and Nolan for a wedding present?" Vic asked.

Morgan shrugged. "I don't know. Want to go in on something together?"

"Yeah. Let's talk tomorrow." Vic replied as he wrapped his arm around Aubrey's waist and pulled her in to his side.

Jealousy speared through him. Ryan wanted to touch Morgan, to show her some affection, but they couldn't do that in public without raising more suspicions. They didn't need anyone knowing what was going on…not yet anyway. He still held out hope they would be announcing their engagement by Christmas. The ring was ready, *he* was ready. He just needed Morgan to be ready.

How could he protect his legacy if the relationship remained one-sided?

"I hope Heath stays away tonight," Ryan added. "He's caused enough of a scandal and folks just want to focus on having a good time and looking ahead to the holidays."

Vic nodded. "He'll be at the wedding next weekend. He's Nolan's best man."

"As long as Chelsea and Nolan's day isn't ruined, that's all that matters," Morgan told them.

Vic took a sip from his drink of choice and glanced around the spacious ballroom. "Jayden's here. I need to talk to him."

Morgan's brother slid his hand into Aubrey's as he eased her away. "If you both will excuse us."

Ryan nodded and once he was alone again with Morgan, he still kept his distance. Playing this part was ridiculous, but necessary. He wanted to get them over that hump and to the other side where they could be free and didn't have to hide any aspect of their relationship or the child they'd created.

"Is this just as awkward and difficult for you as it is for me?" she asked on a sigh, clearly frustrated.

Ryan slid his hands into his pockets. "These clothes are damn uncomfortable, but yes. In the past week, I haven't kept this much distance between us and I'm starting to get cranky."

Morgan stepped forward and motioned toward the dance floor. "Then let's have that dance now," she suggested. "Even friends dance together, right?"

He moved to close the distance between them, still not touching her, but close enough to see those bright blue eyes and the navy flecks. Her familiar floral perfume enveloped him, pulling him in even deeper. He'd grown so accustomed to everything about Morgan that he couldn't imagine trying to build a life with anyone else. This just made sense on so many levels.

"Is that where we are?" Ryan purposely dropped his gaze to her painted red lips, then back up. "Friends?"

"I don't know what label to put on us, honestly," she confessed on a whisper. "I know that I want to dance with you and then I want to go back home and let you fulfill that promise of peeling this dress off me."

"I like that you refer to the ranch as home."

He hadn't heard her say that before, and he wondered how long she'd thought of Yellow Rose as hers. Or maybe that was just a slip of the tongue. Regardless, he could tell she'd gotten comfortable at the ranch and he could easily see her there long-term with their child…and maybe more.

One step at a time, though. He had to win her over first.

When he'd built that house and started his life there, he had designed everything around his future and the family he would ultimately have.

Morgan didn't say a word. She just offered a sweet smile as she turned and headed for the dance floor. They could talk about her thoughts of calling the ranch her home later. Right now, he wanted to dance with the woman he planned on spending his life with. Ryan followed those swaying hips at a distance and hoped he didn't appear too eager.

"I'm not sure I could've pulled this off without you by my side. Thank you."

Morgan stared down at the spread of food and bit her lip.

"You did it. I just supervised," Nelson assured her. "Ryan is a simple man. He likes meat and potatoes. You couldn't go wrong."

Morgan snorted. "Oh, I can go very wrong in the kitchen," she assured him. "But having your guidance gave me confidence."

Nelson patted her shoulder. "Ryan has never brought a woman to the ranch to stay, and just the fact you want to help and learn about his favorite meals really says a great deal about this relationship. Dare I hope this is serious?"

Having a man's baby was pretty serious, but even beyond that, Morgan had fallen for the man when she swore she wouldn't get more involved. Yet here she was, learning tips from Ryan's chef and waiting for him to come in from the pastures.

Morgan had called Nelson and asked him to come in on his day off. With her shop in good hands with Kylie, this was the perfect day for a surprise because Ryan never took days off from Yellow Rose. She couldn't wait to see the look on his face if she actually managed to pull this off.

"I'm not sure where we are right now," she answered Nelson honestly. "But I do love it here."

She wanted the conversation off the relationship and onto anything else.

Morgan faced the elderly man and smiled. "I really do appreciate you coming in on a Sunday. I'm sure you had other things to do like spend time with your family."

"My wife is likely at home quilting and enjoying some movie." His own grin had the wrinkles around his eyes creasing deeper. "I promise, she doesn't mind one bit. After nearly fifty years of marriage, you realize what really matters. She has her hobbies and I have mine. Cooking never feels like work and I love that you wanted to surprise Ryan."

Fifty years of marriage. Morgan couldn't even fathom fifty days, let alone years. That had to be one of the strongest bonds Morgan had ever heard of and she suddenly found herself wanting that deep connection. But how? A one-night stand hardly seemed the firm foundation for a lifelong commitment. Although they had moved beyond all the bickering they used to do. Maybe they'd made some substantial progress. Maybe she could start trusting the evolution of this relationship.

The alarm from the back door chimed through the house and the familiar sound of cowboy boots echoing off the hardwoods filtered into the open kitchen and living area. Morgan didn't know if she was more nervous or excited to show Ryan what she'd done. Well, what she and Nelson had done.

When Ryan rounded the corner, he stopped just on the other side of the island and stared at Morgan, then Nelson.

"Aren't you off today?" Ryan asked. Then his attention went to the various dishes on the counter. "Damn. I knew something smelled amazing when I walked in."

"Miss Morgan wanted to surprise you with your favorites," Nelson explained. "So she called me and I came to give her a quick lesson in the kitchen."

Ryan removed his hat as his eyes landed on her. "Is that right?" he asked with a grin.

There went those silly, naive jitters racing through her simply because the man smiled at her. She was carrying his child, they'd been intimate multiple times, and they were temporarily living together, yet the sweetest gesture somehow stirred up her emotions.

"If you don't need me anymore, I'll head out and let you two enjoy your dinner," Nelson told them.

Morgan couldn't help herself. She reached out and gave the elderly man a hug.

"You are the best," she told him, then eased back. "I can't thank you enough."

"No thanks necessary. I love what I do."

Nelson untied his apron and started to head toward the back door, but stopped and turned to face Ryan.

"You've got something special in that one," he stated, nodding toward Morgan.

Without another word, he left. Once again, the chime echoed as the door opened and closed. Morgan rested her hands on the top of the island and stared across at Ryan. He still had that silly grin and she couldn't help but smile back.

"I have no idea what made you want to do this, but it all looks amazing."

Morgan shrugged. "You've done so much for me and you're so busy. I don't know, I just wanted to do something to show you that I appreciate how much you've made me feel at home here."

Ryan started to circle the island, his gaze never wavering from hers. Morgan shifted to face him and when he kept advancing, she backed up until she hit the edge of the counter. Ryan leaned in, and his hands came to rest on either side of her hips.

"You smell like the barn." She laid her hands against his chest and laughed.

Ryan leaned in even closer. "You don't care," he murmured against her lips. "You might be prissy with your specialty clothes, but deep down, you're still a rancher at heart."

"I'm not," she argued.

"You love it here," he countered. "You told me so multiple times. I think you just needed a ranch where you could put your stamp on it."

Those bright blue eyes held her in place and had her heart quickening and breath caught in her throat.

"I haven't put my stamp here."

Ryan's low laugh sent a warmth spreading through her. "I assure you I wouldn't have put Christmas decorations up on my house or extra trees inside. I wouldn't have cleared out an extra stall for you to have a horse of your own if you want, and I never would have come in so early from working today had you not been here. Your stamp is everywhere."

She supposed that might be true, but she hadn't thought of things in that way before. She hadn't realized just how deeply she'd fallen into the ranch because she'd been too consumed with falling into the man.

Morgan slid her hands on up to his shoulders. "Your food is getting cold and I worked too hard for you to not enjoy it fresh."

Ryan nipped at her lips. "I'd rather enjoy other things right now."

Oh, this man knew exactly what to say to distract her and make her mind believe that this temporary setup could be something long-term.

But he'd never said anything about loving her or wanting something beyond building his legacy and raising the next generation of Carters.

"Let's eat first," she told him. "Then you can enjoy me however you want."

Ryan groaned and dropped his head, then took a step back.

"I really can't believe you called in Nelson for a cooking lesson."

Morgan crossed her arms and pulled in a deep breath, trying to focus after that promise of the extracurricular activities coming soon.

"I really didn't know what else to do for you and I'm not the best cook, so I thought I'd try. Who knows, maybe I'll like cooking and can whip up something on Nelson's days off. Don't count on that, but if we can go from fighting like crazy, then maybe I'll like cooking for us."

Ryan's brows rose as his eyes widened. "You're staying here?"

Morgan chewed her bottom lip and weighed her next words carefully. "I haven't made up my mind, but I'm not in a hurry to go just yet."

The way he smiled, like he knew something she didn't, had Morgan shaking her head.

"Don't get so cocky, now," she warned. "I didn't agree to anything. I just said I was staying awhile and thinking about this. The baby has to eat, too."

Ryan glanced to the mashed potatoes, baked steak, rolls, asparagus wrapped in bacon, and a chocolate cake and then back to her.

He quirked brow. "Interesting that all of this is my favorite."

"Yeah, well, I started with your favorites as a way to say thank you for all you've done," she told him. "But that doesn't mean I'm staying, so stop looking at me that way."

"If you want to get naked, I can look at you a different way," he retorted.

Morgan smacked his chest. "Go sit down and I'll get us some plates."

He snaked an arm around her waist and pulled her close. "You go sit. You made the meal, the least I could do is serve you."

"Serve me? I do like the sound of that."

His lips feathered lightly over hers as his hand slid down to her backside. "I'll be serving you later, too."

A thrill shot through Morgan and she wondered if she would always have this feeling of excitement where Ryan was concerned. Was it just the fast-paced new scenario she'd found that made her so giddy? Or was there something much deeper that she should try to hold on to?

Her month was quickly coming to an end and she might just stick around a little longer to see where this all would lead.

Eighteen

Ryan didn't know why he was so nervous. This wasn't his wedding day, but since Morgan mentioned staying longer, that was all his mind could process.

Their conversation almost a week ago had him in knots. He wanted her to stay. He wanted to put that ring on her finger so they could start their life with the family they'd created.

And that was why he couldn't concentrate on anything else. He was giving Morgan this important day with her sister and then he would present her the ring to let her know just how serious he was. He knew she was starting to think about long-term and he couldn't let this opportunity pass. The entire future of Yellow Rose was on the line.

Ryan waited in the line of people entering the Texas Cattleman's Club. The doorways and railings had garlands and flowers draped and wrapped all over. As soon as he stepped inside, he felt as if he'd been transformed into something from a magazine with all the white and lights with touches of gold. The clubhouse had even more Christmas decor than it had last weekend for the Christmas party...and he hadn't even thought that was possible.

Evergreen trees lit up in groupings were all around the perimeter. The white cloth-covered chairs sat in neat little rows facing the stage in the main ball-room. The place was likely Chelsea's dream wed-ding come true.

Ryan wondered what type of wedding Morgan would want. Did she want something over-the-top and flashy, or would she be more low-key and want something on her family ranch? Or his ranch?

A wedding at Yellow Rose would be ideal for him, but he had to take this all one step at a time. Morgan wasn't even wearing his ring yet.

He wished they could have arrived together, but she had been with her sisters and the rest of the bridal party getting their hair and makeup done. He hadn't seen her dress or how she looked. He'd left her sleep-ing in bed this morning and had gone to the stable to check on his mare that was still recovering from a stillbirth. Morgan had been gone when he'd re-turned hours later.

When he wasn't with her, there was always a sliver

of anticipation as to when he would again. What would she look like? Would she meet his gaze and offer a sultry smile? Why did he have these school-aged emotions and excitement each time he thought of Morgan?

Ryan found a seat toward the middle, but closer to the aisle. He wanted to see Morgan coming down. He wanted to catch her attention. He wanted her to constantly be thinking of him the way he was her.

As Ryan glanced around and nodded to a few people he knew, he couldn't help but wonder how many of these folks would be in attendance at his and Morgan's wedding. Because there was no way in hell he could let her go now.

Morgan knew Ryan was staring at her. Anytime she stole a glance in the direction of the guests, there he sat with those bright blue eyes locked onto her.

Although, knowing Ryan, he was likely staring at her chest because Morgan had a serious fear that one good inhale and she'd bust this zipper. Her breasts were so swollen even though her belly still showed no signs of the pregnancy. She actually couldn't wait and every day when she woke up, she stared in the mirror and turned to the side hoping to see something.

Morgan focused on her sister's vows and then Nolan's. The two were so perfect for each other as they stared into each other's eyes with their hands joined. Chelsea had been so excited to get down the aisle, she had been beaming all morning and afternoon. She was finally getting to marry the man of her dreams and live the life she'd always wanted. She couldn't believe both her sisters were married.

A heavy dose of remorse and sadness swept through her as she stood at her sister's side. This was everything Morgan didn't know she wanted. Not just the gorgeous flowing gown and the perfect bouquet and decor. But the love, the adoration they showed each other, the solidarity that could only come from such an unbreakable bond.

Morgan wanted that and she wanted it all with Ryan.

She glanced his way once again and he offered her a crooked grin that melted her heart. She'd never experienced these feelings with anyone else and she had no idea how he would respond to her truth. But she had to tell him. Ryan deserved to know and Morgan deserved this chance at happiness.

She wanted to say yes to his proposal, but she couldn't go that far without telling him she loved him first.

This would be the riskiest move she ever made and his response would change the course on her path of life. If he rejected her, she would move back to the Grandin ranch and they would have to coparent, but if he accepted her love and offered his in return, she knew they would have a beautiful life together at Yellow Rose. But she couldn't marry him if the love only existed on her side. An unbalanced relationship would surely crumble and that was a risk she couldn't take.

When the minister proclaimed Chelsea and Nolan were husband and wife, everyone in attendance clapped as the newlyweds shared their first kiss. Tears pricked Morgan's eyes. She smiled as Layla handed Chelsea's heavy bouquet back to her.

This is exactly what Morgan could have if she went after it…and she had every intention of going after Ryan Carter.

After the pictures outside the clubhouse and a few inside, Morgan looped her arm through Heath's as they made their way back into the ballroom with the rest of the wedding party. She wanted a quick word before the party began.

"I hope we can bury all of this between our families and focus on your brother and my sister," she told him. "I know that there has been so much animosity and anger, but it's time to move on."

Heath scoffed. "I will do whatever it takes to honor my mother's and Ashley's memory. Surely you can understand my position and that I have no hard feelings toward you, but I have to do something to make things right."

Well, that made her wonder about his next move, but Morgan refused to get into it with him at the reception. There would be a time and a place to tackle Heath Thurston, and maybe now that Nolan was married into the Grandin family, he could talk his twin into giving up this vendetta.

Heath guided her to the reception table with the rest of the party. "Family is everything to me," he

added in a low tone as he inched toward her. "I'm
sure even the Grandins can appreciate that."

Morgan leaned away from him. Now that Heath
knew the truth about his mother being paid off with
those rights, he seemed even angrier, which could be
dangerous. What did he have planned now?

Morgan hoped more than anything that Chelsea
and Nolan could have a fresh start without this black
cloud of scandal hovering over them.

Morgan took a seat and immediately searched for
where Ryan would be. She nearly laughed when she
spotted him at the bar holding his tumbler of bourbon and Sylvia standing right beside him with her
hands moving all around as she chattered, no doubt
about some town gossip.

The poor guy stared back at her and looked like he
wanted to be rescued. Considering she was his *friend*,
Morgan would do just that.

She scooted her chair back and gathered her
emerald-green skirt in one hand. The entire back
part of the ballroom had been set up for the reception and was even more breathtaking than Morgan
had imagined. There was something magical and almost hopeful about a Christmas wedding.

The soft music filled the room and the twinkling
lights, the suspended lanterns, the tall adorned trees
surrounding the perimeter all had such a romantic
ambiance. Maybe she should ask Ryan to dance and
tell him. She didn't want to wait to open her heart to
him. So many emotions had been building inside her,

and she hadn't realized until today just how much love she had for him.

And all this time, she'd never believed in such a commitment. She'd thought that was only for fairy tales, but there were too many of her family members and friends in this town falling in love, and Morgan had to believe that type of commitment truly did exist when you found the right person.

And she had found her person.

"Sylvia, you do look amazing just like I knew you would."

Sylvia turned to face Morgan and propped a hand on her rounded hip. "Well, thank you. I absolutely love this gown you chose for me. And, honey, you are radiant in that green dress."

Morgan shot a look to Ryan, and his smile and locked stare silently said he agreed. She loved the way he looked at her. It made her feel both sexy and beautiful. He had a way of doing things to her emotions and desires and he didn't even have to say a word.

"Thank you," Morgan replied.

"I was just going to get a champagne," Sylvia stated. "Can I get you one, dear?"

Morgan's breath caught in her throat and before she could reply, Ryan chimed in.

"The wedding party already has champagne at their table."

Yes. That was actually true, but she'd been so stunned that she hadn't thought of the logical reply.

Clearly Morgan's nerves and thoughts were all over the place.

"Thank you anyway," she told Sylvia.

When Sylvia turned toward the bartender to order, Morgan gave a slight nod for Ryan to follow her. She had to stop herself from reaching for his hand and remember they were in a very public venue.

She hoped soon they would be able to go public with their love and their news of the baby. She hoped the folks of the town would embrace all that had happened in a positive way.

Chelsea stepped into view and Morgan startled as she reached for her sister's arm.

"Sorry," Chelsea stated. "I just wanted to catch you real quick. We're going to do the toast in about ten minutes. So that will be the speeches from Layla and Heath. Make sure you're back at the table."

Morgan had helped Layla rehearse her speech over and over all day. She truly wanted this day to be everything Chelsea had envisioned and dreamed of. Layla would do a great job.

"I'll be there," she assured her sister.

Chelsea's eyes shifted over Morgan's shoulder, and Chelsea merely smiled before she moved on to mingle with other guests. The DJ continued to play a nice mix of popular hits and slow love songs, perfect for the reception and dancing.

When she turned to talk to Ryan, she noticed his sights were not on her, but on Heath over near the entrance talking to Nolan.

"What did he tell you?" Ryan asked without taking his focus off Heath.

"Oh, just talking about taking what belonged to his mother and how he would do anything for his family. Don't worry about it. We'll deal with him another day."

Ryan's gaze darted her direction. "I don't trust him and I don't want him near you or our child."

"He won't hurt me," she assured him. "I think he's just upset by the fact that even his own surveyor hasn't been successful. He's lashing out and right now everyone is his target."

"Not you. Never you."

Ryan turned away and before Morgan realized what he was doing, he was across the room and standing before Heath. Morgan couldn't run after him or she'd look like the concerned girlfriend, but she did casually make her way over in time to hear Ryan deliver a threat.

"Morgan Grandin is off-limits to whatever new game you're playing."

Heath sneered. "And who are you to Morgan?"

"A friend," Ryan fired back. "Just keep your distance from her."

Heath raised a brow and glanced directly to her. "I'm not after anyone. I'm only here to take what was promised to my mother."

Nolan stepped between them and placed a hand on his brother's chest. "Let's all relax and save this argument for another day."

Ryan took a step back. "There's nothing more to discuss. Heath will keep his distance from Morgan."

"Again, why the hell do you care so much?" Heath volleyed back. "Unless you and Morgan are more than friends."

"Just friends," Ryan ground out. "I protect those I care about, as you can appreciate given your stance."

Ryan spun on his heel and Morgan had to step aside as he marched away. She didn't know whether to be mortified at the scene that had been made at her sister's wedding or let that blossom of hope bloom at the fact Ryan said he cared for her.

Morgan offered Nolan a soft smile before she walked away, as well. In an attempt to keep up the friend persona for the public, she had to give Ryan a bit of space, but not too much. She wanted nothing more than to go to him, but she needed to give him time.

The next slow song that came on, she'd approach him and ask for a dance. They needed to calm down, to decompress and remember nothing else mattered right now but them and their baby.

If she could get him in an intimate embrace, they would have a few minutes to talk. She needed to see where he was in his head and tell him how much she'd fallen for him to see if there was any chance at all at their own happily-ever-after.

Nineteen

Ryan wished like hell he hadn't gotten so set off, but the mere idea of Heath Thurston talking to Morgan had not only made him jealous, Ryan wondered if he was still a threat to her family. He didn't like Heath's body language as they spoke. Ryan wanted to guard and keep Morgan safe from any more emotional upheaval.

Regardless of the encounter, Ryan didn't like it. He'd never been a jealous man, but seeing Heath arm in arm with Morgan walking back into the clubhouse after the photos had already put him in a bad mood. Maybe his protective streak intertwined with the jealousy, but either way, he wanted to keep Morgan in a bubble.

When she told him that Heath still mentioned getting what belonged to his mother, that was all Ryan needed to snap and step in to make sure she knew she didn't have to face anything alone.

"Dance with me."

The slow ballad filled the ballroom, and Ryan turned to see Morgan standing before him. That emerald-green strapless gown hugged her every curve and enhanced her bust in a way that made Ryan want to say to hell with what people thought. He wanted to grab her and dance the way he craved, with her body pressed firmly against his. He didn't want to have to worry about hand placement or if he grazed his lips over hers.

Did he want too much? Were these feelings more than he could handle right now? He liked to think he could take on anything, but even this avenue was new to him. He'd thought he'd been in love before… but look where that got him.

The moment they hit the floor, Ryan took Morgan's hand and pulled her into a dance. That long red hair curled down over one shoulder and those expressive blue eyes met his. She was the most striking woman he'd ever seen in his life and she was his— temporarily.

"Forget about Heath."

Morgan's words penetrated his thoughts and he shook his head. "I was actually thinking about how hot you looked in this dress, but he's still on my mind. I don't like that bastard."

"I didn't ask you to make friends with him, I asked you to forget about him," she stated with a firm tone.

Ryan nodded. "I get it, but I didn't like…"

Damn it. He sounded like a fool for admitting what he'd been thinking or how he'd felt earlier.

"You didn't like what?" she prodded.

He spun her around and dodged other dancing couples and tried to keep his voice low.

"I didn't like seeing you walking together, all right?"

A slow smile spread across Morgan's face. "You're jealous?"

"Go ahead, laugh about it."

"Oh, I'm not laughing," she corrected him as her hand tightened in his when he spun her once again. "I'm letting that nugget of information sink in."

The way she kept grinning at him like she had some special secret had him both worried and turned on. Nothing lit up a space more than Morgan's smile, but there was a little smirk there that didn't sit well with him.

"You've got something on your mind," he murmured. "What are you thinking that has you so happy?"

"I just never thought you'd love me the way I love you," she told him, her hands coming to rest on his shoulders. "I thought I'd have to tell you first and you'd run in the other direction."

Ryan stilled and brought them to a stop.

"What did you say?" he asked.

"I love you." Her smile got even wider and her

eyes filled with unshed tears. "I never knew how liberating that would be to say. I never knew how right those words would feel. But knowing you love me back…"

Ryan's heart clenched as he tried to find his words and absorb the bomb she'd just dropped into his world.

"I never said I loved you," he corrected her. "That's not where I am, Morgan."

That smile faltered slowly until it completely vanished. Her hands slid down his chest and dropped to her sides.

"What do you mean?" she asked. "You just said that you didn't like seeing me walking with another man. You're jealous and the way you've been going all out at the house… How can you say that's not love?"

"Because it's not."

He refused to allow his mind to even go there. He'd tried that years ago and had been left standing with nothing. No family, no emotions. He'd vowed to never allow his heart to go there ever again.

"Then what is it?" she asked, her lips thinned as a lone tear slid down her cheek.

Ryan tried to reach for her, but she held her hands up and took a step back. He didn't want to make a scene, but right now all that mattered was Morgan and her emotions.

"I don't want to hurt you," he added. "I just have to be honest."

She let out a humorless laugh and swiped at the moisture on her face. "I guess you were honest all along. You told me from the beginning you only wanted to marry me for the baby."

Ryan cringed at that last word that came out just as one slow song ended and another began. The ill-timed statement drew the attention of everyone around them.

As if Morgan just realized what she'd said, she glanced around them. Ryan spotted Vic and Aubrey, Nolan and Chelsea, Jayden and Zanai, Sylvia and a whole host of other guests.

Ryan wished like hell he could turn back time and slip out the side door to talk to Morgan. But he'd had no clue whatsoever that she would reveal her love for him. When she'd mentioned staying with him, he assumed it was for the family, nothing more.

After a moment of awkward silence and tension swirling around them, Chelsea stepped forward and touched Morgan's elbow.

"Why don't you two take this to one of the other rooms?" she suggested.

Morgan turned her attention to her sister. "Chels, my word, I'm so sorry. I didn't mean—"

"I know. It's a tough time, but you need privacy."

Morgan nodded and gathered the skirt of her dress and headed out the ballroom.

Chelsea glanced to Ryan. "If you're not going to love her like she deserves, then let her go."

She turned from him and went back to her new husband, who was also glaring at Ryan.

Somehow being honest had gotten him in trouble, but he didn't have the time, nor did he care what anyone else thought. He'd hurt Morgan and that was all that mattered at this point. He would never intentionally harm her, so now he had to make sure she knew exactly where he stood.

Ryan headed out the ballroom and found her down the hall near the women's rec center. She stood with her back to him and as he approached, he had no idea if his touch would be welcome or if she'd jerk away.

Ryan reached for her anyway and laid a hand on her shoulder.

"Look at me."

She turned, and the soft glow from all the Christmas lights and the wall sconces illuminated the dampness on her cheeks. But there was more than just the tears. There was a pain and vulnerability in her eyes he'd never seen before.

"You don't need to say a word," she told him. "You never promised me anything and you said more than once that you only wanted to raise a family with me for the sake of your legacy. You made it perfectly clear that the baby was the reason for the marriage."

"I had no idea that you had stronger feelings," he explained. "You had told me you didn't believe in love."

"I didn't. Until you."

Guilt weighed heavy on his heart because Morgan was the last person he would ever want to break.

"Morgan—"

"No." She held up a hand and pasted on a smile

he knew had to be tearing her apart. "We both know where we stand now and I don't want to ruin any more of my sister's day. I need to get back inside and listen to Layla's speech."

Ryan blinked. "You're going back in after everyone just found out about our baby?"

Morgan shrugged. "Why hide now? The secret is out, and just because my life is falling apart doesn't mean my sister's should. She's counting on me."

Morgan started to move around him, but he reached for her. His fingers curled just inside her arm and her gaze met his.

"We can talk back at the house."

Morgan closed her eyes and blew out a sigh before meeting his gaze once again. "We're done talking, Ryan. We're just…done."

And then she was gone, leaving Ryan standing in the hallway with a broken heart. He had no clue how the hell that had happened when he didn't even know his heart had been involved.

From the beginning, he'd vowed to win this challenge, to have her marry him. Now he realized the most important component had been Morgan all along. Not winning or losing.

And discovering that truth after the fact was how he'd lost everything.

Twenty

Morgan hadn't been back to the ranch in three days. She'd ignored Ryan's calls and texts, and thankfully he hadn't stopped in to her store. She had needed time to process everything that had happened, not that she thought she'd get over him in a few days. But she'd needed space to gather her thoughts before she approached him again.

She'd gone back to living at the family ranch and working all day at her business and realized just how empty her life was without Ryan. No shared dinners or fun flirting followed by a night of passion. There was no deep conversations that made her heart feel so alive. Even with her parents' support, the nights were still quiet. The silence seemed to mock her decision to tell Ryan her true feelings. Had she said nothing and just agreed to marry him, she'd still have him.

That wouldn't have been fair to either of them, though. She had never settled for anything in life, and refused to let her marriage be the first. Clearly, Ryan was still hell-bent on having his nuptials mean little more than a business deal.

This new chapter was something she was just going to have to get used to and deal with the best way she knew how. Living without Ryan would be her new normal. Even though she had only been at the ranch three weeks, that had been long enough to get her hopes up and make her want a real life with Ryan and not something out of obligation.

Unfortunately, she had to go back to the ranch to get her things. There was no way around it and she couldn't avoid Ryan forever. They were having a child and they'd just have to figure out how to get along.

And that was how she found herself sitting in her car, staring up at the Christmas lights dotting all the peaks and porches of Ryan's home. She'd been so happy and surprised the day he'd done that. The joy from that memory was now overshadowed by the pain of the loss.

She just wanted to get this all over with and go back to her house.

Morgan stepped from her car and pulled her jacket tighter around her. Supposedly there was a storm moving in…snow, of all things. That was just absurd in this area of Texas, but at this point, a freak snow-storm was the least of her worries.

The frigid wind cut right through her as she headed toward the front door and rang the bell. How silly was that? Just days ago this had been her home, a place where she'd envisioned living the rest of her life, yet now she stood outside ringing the bell because she was just a guest.

The foyer light flicked on and a moment later, Ryan opened the door. He didn't appear surprised to see her. If anything, he looked miserable.

"There's no need to ring the damn bell," he grumbled. "Come in."

Morgan stepped inside and took notice of his appearance. Messy hair, wrinkled tee, jeans, no shoes. He was still typical Ryan, but this version seemed sadder and frustrated. Well, welcome to the club.

"I just need to gather my things. I have quite a bit, so I can get a load now and come back tomorrow and finish," she informed him. "I don't want to be in your way."

She would not ask for his help. She didn't want him in her bedroom touching her stuff and packing like she was just going on a trip. She was leaving…for good.

"In my way?" he scoffed. "You've been in my way for months. You're in my head, in my space, you're everywhere in my damn house even when you aren't physically here."

Morgan blinked at his harsh tone, but remained still. Clearly, he was irritated, but right now she couldn't tell if it was at her or himself.

"Don't move out."

She jerked, knowing she'd heard him wrong because they'd already been over this. She'd told him she loved him and he didn't reciprocate the feelings. Sticking around now would only prolong the pain and the inevitable.

"Give this more time," he told her. "Give *us* more time."

"For what?" she countered. "We are at opposite ends of the emotional spectrum and the gap is too large to meet in the middle. Neither of us should settle for something we don't want."

When he stood there staring, the silence became too much, and Morgan shifted around him to head up the stairs. There was no point in dragging this out any longer than necessary. The pain wouldn't be erased in a day and they both just needed time.

The most important thing now would be to put the baby's foundation first. Morgan's broken heart and whatever Ryan was dealing with would just have to take a step back.

Morgan reached the bedroom she'd started out in before moving to Ryan's. Her clothes and personal belongings were still in the spare room.

As soon as she opened the door, there stood that damn tree. Why did every memory here have to be so amazing and wonderful? Why did he have to leave such an impression on her heart? Because she knew deep down that he'd ruined her for absolutely everyone else.

The sooner she got her things, the sooner she could

leave. Staying here and traveling down memory lane would only hurt her further.

She stared at all of her makeup and brushes on the vanity and pulled in a deep breath.

"I don't want to meet in the middle."

Morgan glanced to the doorway, where Ryan seemed to fill up the entire space.

"What?" she asked.

"You said the gap was too large for us to meet in the middle," he clarified. "I don't want to be in the middle. I want to be on the other side…with you."

Tired and more than frustrated, Morgan sank down onto her plush vanity stool. She rested her elbow on the counter and rubbed her head as she tried to gather her thoughts and make sense of how they got here.

"I don't even know what you're trying to say," she told him. "How can you be with me when you don't love me? I told you I wouldn't settle and I meant it."

Ryan stepped forward and bent down to look her in the eye, resting his hands on her thighs. His gaze held hers and she'd never seen such raw emotion staring back at her as she did right now.

"I don't want you to settle," he explained. "It wasn't fair for me to ask you to or just assume you would."

What was he trying to say? She didn't want to get her hopes up, not again, but there was that spark of hope igniting inside her. She didn't want to say anything. She needed to let him guide this conversation.

"These past few days have been hell," he went on. "Do you know how damn lonely this house was without you? All of these Christmas decorations seemed so cheerful and all I could think of was how much you loved them. You loved from the beginning with your whole heart and I never saw it. I'm not sure you saw it either until recently. But that's who you are, Morgan. You just shine with love and you showed me that it's okay to open my heart again."

Tears pricked her eyes as her throat clogged with emotions.

"What are you saying?" she whispered.

He shifted onto one knee and pulled something from his pocket. A box.

Her heart clenched as she gasped.

"Marry me," he said as he lifted the lid to reveal a stunning diamond with smaller stones along the band. "I've had this since the day after you told me about the baby, but the timing was never right. Now is the time."

Why did life have to be so cruel? This hurt more than walking away. To know she could have it all right now if she said yes, but she wouldn't really have it all…would she?

"I'm still not settling," she reminded him. "We're obviously both miserable, but that doesn't change the fact I fell in love with you, Ryan."

"I fell in love with you, too."

Morgan stilled. "What?"

Tears gathered in his eyes as well, and her heart flipped over in her chest. This was truly happening for her—for them.

"I fell in love with you," he repeated. "Maybe that

first night we were together, maybe when you told me about the baby, or maybe when I hung those damn lights on the house. I don't know when it happened because I was too afraid to admit it to myself, let alone you. But being here without you was a hell of a lot worse than exposing my vulnerability and taking this risk."

He took the ring from the box and lifted her hand. His eyes met hers once again.

"I'm asking you to marry me now for all the right reasons." He slid the ring on, and held her hand and sniffled, obviously trying to hold back his own emotions. "I'm asking you because we love each other, because we have a child who deserves the best home, and because I want to build something bigger here with you than either of us ever imagined. I know you might find my words difficult to believe, but I wouldn't fight so hard if I didn't love you so damn much."

Morgan laughed as tears slid down her cheeks. She glanced to the ring that fit so perfectly and looked exactly like something she would choose.

"Yes," she told him. "I want to build everything with you from here on out."

Ryan let out a sigh and reached for her, wrapping his arms around her and resting his forehead against hers.

"I thought I had ruined everything," he whispered. "I can't handle the thought of you not with me forever. It scared the hell out of me."

Yeah, this man definitely loved her and three days of misery was worth the lesson they'd both learned.

Morgan framed his face with her hands and eased back to stare him in the eyes. "I guess we have more to announce to the town than just our baby."

Ryan smiled, then covered her lips with his for a brief kiss.

"What do you say we make our announcement at the New Year's Eve ball?" he suggested. "Since we're known for our public statements."

Morgan couldn't help but laugh. "I love that idea and I love you."

He nipped her lips once again. "Love you more. We might be stubborn and butt heads, but there's nobody else I'd want to do that with than you."

Morgan knew deep in her heart this was just the beginning of that grand dynasty Ryan wanted for his family. Day one of the rest of their lives had a beautiful ring to it.

* * * * *

When Heath is trapped in a snowstorm with a beauty, will she change his beastly heart? Find out in the final installment of Texas Cattleman's Club: Ranchers and Rivals

Rancher After Midnight
by Karen Booth

Available next month!

#2917 RANCHER AFTER MIDNIGHT
Texas Cattleman's Club: Ranchers and Rivals
by Karen Booth
Rancher Heath Thurston built his entire life around vengeance. But Ruby Bennett's tender heart and passionate kisses are more than a match for his steely armor. Anything can happen on New Year's...even a hardened man's chance at redemption!

#2918 HOW TO CATCH A COWBOY
Hartmann Heirs • by Katie Frey
Rodeo rider Jackson Hartmann wants to make a name for himself without Hartmann connections. Team masseuse Hannah Bean has family secrets of her own. Working together on the rodeo circuit might mean using *all* his seductive cowboy wiles to win her over...

#2919 ONE NIGHT ONLY
Hana Trio • by Jayci Lee
Thanks to violinist Megan Han's one-night fling with her father's new CFO, Daniel Pak, she's pregnant! No one can know the truth—especially not her matchmaking dad, who would demand marriage. If only her commitment-phobic, not-so-ex lover would open his heart...

#2920 THE TROUBLE WITH LOVE AND HATE
Sweet Tea and Scandal • by Cat Schield
Teagan Burns will do anything to create her women's shelter, but developer Chase Love stands in the way. When these enemies find themselves on the same side to save a historic Charleston property, sparks fly. But will diverging goals tear them apart?

#2921 THE BILLIONAIRE PLAN
The Image Project • by Katherine Garbera
Delaney Alexander will do anything to bring down her underhanded ex—even team up with his biggest business rival, Nolan Cooper. But soon the hot single-dad billionaire has her thinking more about forever than payback...

#2922 HER BEST FRIEND'S BROTHER
Six Gems • by Yahrah St. John
Travel blogger Wynter Barrington has always crushed on her brother's best friend. Then a chance encounter with Riley Davis leads to a steamy affair. Will the notorious playboy take a chance on love...or add Riley to his list of heartbreaks?

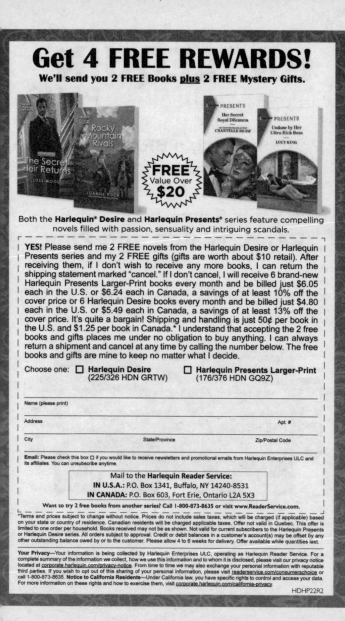

HARLEQUIN
PLUS

Announcing a **BRAND-NEW**
multimedia subscription service
for romance fans like you!

Read, Watch and Play.

Experience the easiest way to get
the romance content you crave.

Start your **FREE 7 DAY TRIAL** at
<u>www.harlequinplus.com/freetrial</u>.